The Landers Mystique

The Mason Braithwaite Paranormal
Mystery Series, book 13

In this series:

Signs Point to Yes

The Desert Rats

Reach for the Sky

Billy Blood

Rubber–Band Ball

The Invisible Arrow

Penstock Canyon

The Man from Grapalia

The Mythical Blond

Stealth Glasses

The Melted Pineapple

Night on the Water

The Landers Mystique

DAGMARMIURA.COM

The Landers Mystique

The Landers Mystique

Christopher Church

DAGMAR MIURA

LOS ANGELES

Published by Dagmar Miura
Los Angeles
www.dagmarmiura.com

The Landers Mystique

This is a work of fiction. Names, characters, businesses, places, events, and incidents are either the products of the author's imagination or used in a fictitious manner. Any resemblance to actual persons, living or dead, or actual events is purely coincidental.

First published 2021

ISBN: 978-1-951130-47-3

One

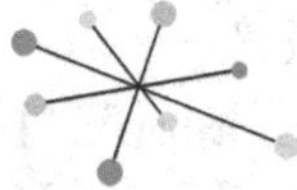

"S HE CALLS IT A ranch house," Matt said, "even though there aren't any animals. It's her country place."

Another professor at Matt's university had offered him the house for a weekend getaway, and now Matt was inviting his girlfriend, Peggy, and her roommates, Mason and Ned. The four of them were sitting around the dinner table, enjoying Ned's *socca*.

"What part of the Mojave is it in?" Ned said.

"Landers. It's close to the flats where the Marine base is, but it still has life around it—Joshua trees and yuccas and cacti."

"I've heard of that place," Mason said. "It's right up the road from Giant Rock. They used to have flying-saucer meet-ups there in the 1950s. But the aliens don't come around anymore."

"Giant Rock was before the little gray aliens," Matt said, waving his fork. "Back then they were called the space brothers. Mostly they looked like effete Swedes."

"Maybe we can leave the paranormal stuff out of it," Ned said, eyeing him. "I get enough exposure in everyday life."

Mason shot him a look. "I don't even tell you half the psychic stuff I do. Your skeptical brain couldn't handle it."

Peggy waved dismissively. "Forget all that. I say we do it. My school gets out at two on Friday."

Matt eyed Mason. "Does the psychic world need you to be in LA this weekend?"

"Things have been slow." Mason leaned back in his chair and ran a hand through his thick red hair. "I can leave whenever."

"So you're not working on any psychic investigations?"

"Nothing that I'm getting paid for."

Ned furrowed his brow in mock concern. "Has there been a disturbance in the unseen world?"

"More like a lack of Angelenos who need my help these days. And it's nothing for you to worry about—I'll make rent."

After they'd eaten, and made some plans for the trip to Landers, Matt left, and Mason helped Peggy clean up. Ned got a pass because he'd made dinner, and he went down the hall to his office.

"It was generous of Matt to invite us too," Mason said, stooping to put the dirty plates in the dishwasher.

Peggy flipped her long hair over her shoulder as she loaded the leftover *socca* into a container. "It'll be more fun with all of us. I get plenty of one-on-one time with Matt. It's why I sent him home tonight."

"I don't mind having him around. He doesn't hog up the bathroom."

"It's not about you. It's good for me to sleep alone sometimes." She pulled open the refrigerator door and set the leftovers inside. "Not that I'm unhappy with Matt. He's great. But once in a while I just need some space."

"The Mojave might be just the ticket, then. It's all about wide open space."

—

ON FRIDAY, GETTING READY for the trip, Mason stood at his side of the closet, flicking through his shirts.

"What kind of clothes do I need?" he called to Ned.

Ned was standing at the foot of their bed,

tucking his own neatly folded clothes into a small duffel bag, already dressed for the road. Mason admired the pleasing contours of his jeans and his stretchy black shirt. Even for a road trip he looked so well put together, his dark Latin hair perfectly coiffed. Mason didn't even bother to try to keep up—no matter what he did, he'd look disheveled almost as soon as he left the house.

"Long sleeves, and jeans, and a sweater," Ned said. "I checked the weather. It still gets cold there at night in April."

Mason was setting his bag beside the front door when Peggy got back from work.

"I don't often see you in jeans," she said, kicking her shoes off. "I guess that's what I'll wear too."

"It seems appropriate," he said, and stepped into the kitchen to see if Ned needed his help packing food. A few minutes later Peggy came back, wearing a T-shirt and denim that flattered her wiry figure.

"I think I'm packed," she said. "What else needs doing?"

"Maybe you could take the food box out," Ned said, "and put it in the trunk. I'm still working on the cooler."

"Let me do that," Mason said. "It's grunt work."

"Not that packing the cooler requires advanced skills," she said.

Mason grinned and slung his bag over one shoulder, then picked up the cardboard box and headed out the front door to the garage. Besides bread and dry pasta and condiments there was a bottle of red wine and a recorked half-empty bottle of white. It was thoughtful of Ned to include booze, considering the guy was dry and in twelve-step. That was one of the things Mason loved about him, his generosity, the way he took care of his friends.

The garage door was up, and the trunk of the Crown Vic was open. Mason set the box in the roomy space and dumped his bag next to it. Scanning the pristine garage, he had to grin. There was only room for Ned's babies, his classic Crown Vic and the 1970s Barracuda, both kept in pristine condition. Mason's bicycle was allowed floor space in one small corner near the side door, but Peggy had to park on the street.

Ned stepped outside with the cooler, followed by Peggy with their bags. As they were loading everything into the trunk, Matt appeared, walking in from the street. As an educator he got away with a relaxed grooming regimen, and today he wore a scruffy week's worth of beard and his brown hair unkempt. He was wearing hiking boots and cargo shorts and a sheer button-up that showed his chest hair.

"When's street sweeping?" he said.

"We'll be back before that," Ned said. "Your car will be fine."

Matt stepped over and loaded his duffel bag into the trunk. "Fuck me—there's still lots of room in here. Peggy must not have put her stuff in yet."

"I resent that," she said, resting her hands on her hips. "Girls don't necessarily have more stuff."

"I'm only taking the basics too," Ned said. "Possessions are a prison."

"So says the guy who has two cars." Matt waved at the trunk. "I still can't believe a woman and two gay guys only have three bags total. And that's all the food? Are you sure it's going to be enough for all of us?"

"Can Matt ride in the trunk?" Peggy said.

"No way—he'd eat our snacks," Ned said. "If that's everything, I'll lock up the house."

"One of you can sit up front," Mason said.

"You're the tall one," Peggy said. "You need the leg room."

"I won't argue." Mason wasn't excessively tall, but with his rugby build, the front seat definitely fit better, and he stepped around to the passenger side.

Once they'd all piled in, and the garage door was closed, Ned navigated down the narrow hillside street to the boulevard, and headed toward the freeway. Traffic was heavy all day on Friday, but Ned maintained his calm driving persona, and soon merged into the carpool lane, east-bound on the 10.

They spent most of the trip chatting as they rolled through the endless urban sprawl. After a couple of hours, when they dropped into the Coachella Valley, the landscape opened up and got interesting. A few minutes later Ned exited the freeway and started the long haul up from the valley floor into the high desert. It was remark-able how much drier it was here, Mason realized, gazing out at the rugged mountainous landscape. They'd left the greenery behind, and he could feel the absence of moisture in the air.

Just as they were cresting the top of the last grade, there was a loud *bang*. Ned eyed the rear-view and quickly hit the brakes, pulling off the highway.

"Was it a tire?" Peggy said.

"It sounded like a gunshot," Ned said, leaning toward Mason to look out the passenger's side.

"This is a town," Matt said, "not the country-side. It's not the kind of place a desert rat would take potshots."

"I don't think it was a gunshot," Mason said. "It was too loud. It's something about your car."

Peggy thumped the back of the seat. "It sounded like it was right behind me."

Ned climbed out, followed by the rest of

them. He studied the rear quarter panel, and the tire, then the rear end.

"No dents or bullet holes."

"Nothing on this side either," Matt said.

Ned opened the trunk, and grabbed the green wine bottle from the food box.

"Look at this. It had a cork in it when I packed it."

Mason felt around among their baggage. "Here's the cork."

"Well, that's a relief." Ned took a deep breath as he wedged it back into the bottle, and then slammed the trunk.

As they climbed back in, Peggy said, "Did it get too hot back there?"

"It's sparkling wine, so there's pressure in the bottle. It blew with the lower air pressure." Ned eyed his side mirror as he pulled back onto the highway.

"And how do we know the air pressure is lower?"

"Well, we just climbed those giant hills. The Coachella Valley is at sea level, and here we're like three thousand feet."

"It's all science," Matt offered. "Higher elevation means lower air pressure."

"You know, my ears might have popped," Mason said, thinking about it as he worked his jaw.

"At least the prosecco didn't spill."

"The most precious cargo of all," Ned said. "Your booze is safe."

The navigation on Ned's phone directed them onto a smaller highway that led onto even higher ground as it wound its way out of the town. The landscape was studded with the peculiar spiky Joshua trees and pinky-tan earth stretching to the rocky hills and distant mountains.

"It's beautiful here," Peggy said, gazing out her window.

"It's not that far from where Gilbert's dad lived," Mason said, "but the landscape is different. What did the homeowner tell you about this place?"

"Her name is Valentina," Matt said. "She says the area is changing because more money is creeping in, and people are renovating and building houses. So it's the same old story as in working-class neighborhoods in the city."

"Gentrification and displacement," Ned said.

"The start of it, anyway. She says that when she thinks of Landers, it's meth-heads and yards full of junked cars."

"Something to look forward to," Ned said.

"Her place isn't like that. There's lots of space around it. You won't have to look at scrapyards."

Ned slowed the car. "The map says I'm supposed to turn off the pavement here."

"It's a dirt road, right?" Matt pulled out his phone. "Valentina says navigation doesn't always pick the best roads from this point."

As they made the turn, Mason eyed the yard on his side of the car, bounded by a chain-link fence, and as predicted, it was jammed full of junked cars. In the corner was a yellowing fiberglass motorboat mounted on a trailer.

"Who needs a boat in the middle of the Mojave?" Peggy said.

Mason gazed at it as they rolled by. "That's what I was wondering."

Ned drove slowly on the uneven surface, and eased up on the accelerator when he hit some washboards, deftly steering around them when he could. Matt guided him through a few more turns, and at one point the road dipped into a small wash, where a patch of pillowy sand had drifted across the tire tracks. Ned sped up as he approached it.

"What are you doing?" Mason said.

"If you don't have four-wheel drive, the only way to get through loose sand is with momentum."

As they crossed it, he could feel the car drifting a little, like a boat on the water. But it was just a few yards, and soon they were through it.

"Well done," Peggy said. "My car would have gotten stuck."

"Your car wouldn't have made it out of the

Coachella Valley," Ned said, eyeing her in the rearview.

"Don't insult my ride."

"I love your ride. It's so cute," he said, and in a falsetto voice, added, "*beep-beep*."

"Mason, your boyfriend is an automotive chauvinist," she said.

"I know what the Joshua trees are," Mason said, gazing out at the landscape, "but what are those bushes all over the place? The ones with the little yellow flowers."

"It's called creosote bush," Matt said. "It grows everywhere out here, high and low. Its range is much more extensive than the Joshua tree."

"So this is Landers?" Ned said. "I haven't really seen a town."

"I think Landers is more a state of mind," Matt said. "There's a post office, so it has a place-name, but it's not really a town."

"This must be Valentina's place," Ned said.

The road ended not far ahead, next to a low structure. As they got closer, Mason could see a set of patio furniture behind it, four iron chairs surrounding a fire pit, next to a tall Joshua tree.

"The directions say the house has red trim along the roof, and a white propane tank on the left."

"Then this is definitely the place," Peggy said. "It's kind of rustic."

Ned pulled up near the front door and killed the engine. "I can see the electric wires, but is there plumbing?"

Matt scoffed. "Of course there's plumbing. There's even internet access."

Mason slung his bag over his shoulder and pulled the cooler out of the trunk. Once Matt had the door open, he followed him into the kitchen and set the cooler on the floor by the refrigerator. Red gingham curtains adorned the windows, and the walls were wood-paneled, with the cabinets in the same blond pine. The kitchen, dining table, and lounge furniture were all in the same big room.

"It feels a bit like Granny's cabin," Ned said, and set to work unloading the cooler.

"At least it's not hoarded out, like the junk-yards we passed."

"The bedrooms are right beside each other," Peggy called from the hallway. "Dibs on the one with the Joshua tree outside the window."

Mason went to look. The bedrooms were the same size, with the same bed, and both had sweeping views of the desert. He dropped his bag on a chair in the corner, then went back out to the car to grab Ned's.

"This fridge is cold," Ned said.

Matt set the cardboard box of food on the counter. "Is that a good thing?"

"It's a very good thing, if you want your romaine to be crisp."

Once they'd settled in, Ned and Peggy set to work on dinner. Mason had to grin—they enjoyed food prep so much that they jumped right into it, even on vacation.

Matt stayed to chat with them, but Mason went into the bedroom, and left the door half open, and stretched out on the bed. Kitchen sounds and muted conversation lulled him toward sleep, but before he drifted off he did a psychic reading of the house and its surroundings.

Folding an arm over his eyes, he cleared his mind, sweeping away the random thoughts that popped up, leaving space for insight to drift in, to suffuse from the edges, from the unseen world. No specific image came to him, but he felt a sense of energy. The air was dry here, and he'd already zapped himself a couple of times with static electricity, when he'd reached for doorknobs and the fridge handle, so maybe feeling a charge wasn't really an extrasensory insight. But the landscape felt like it was energized—a big fresh battery, ready to go.

SOMETIME LATER, NED SHOOK him awake. He was sitting beside him on the bed. "Ready for dinner?"

"Always," Mason mumbled, and sat up.

They'd made a caesar salad and some kind of handmade soy cutlets, breaded and fried, and it was all delicious. The three of them seemed more upbeat, Mason thought, talking and laughing over the food. He felt it too.

"It feels different, doesn't it?" he said. "Being out here."

"I'm definitely feeling lighter," Peggy said. "It's good to get out of town once in a while."

"Cheers to the person who loaned you this house," Ned said, and lifted his water glass.

"To Valentina," Matt said.

"What does she teach?" Mason glanced at him as he forked up more salad.

"She's a biologist too. Her expertise is in lichens and cyanobacteria."

"That sounds a little dry," Ned said. "No wonder she needs a weekend getaway house."

"You'd be amazed how interesting lichens can be. There's a variety out here that only grows under translucent quartz rocks that filter out half the sunlight. It's how they adapted to the desert conditions."

"This really is a unique environment," Mason said. "I can feel it. Like it's supercharged."

Ned waved his fork. "That's not psychic energy. It's just the dryness, and the clean air, and the higher elevation. It all makes your metabolism perk up."

"Dry air is well-known to conduct psychic energy more efficiently," Mason said.

"So there you have it," Peggy said. "A compromise. You're both right."

After they'd finished, twilight was fading, and Mason stepped out the back door, exploring the gravel space that served as a patio. It had grown surprisingly cold, but the chairs and the fire pit looked inviting.

When he stepped back in, Peggy was at the kitchen counter, pouring herself a glass of the prosecco.

"Are we going to sit out there?"

"You'll need a sweater," Mason said, and went to the bedroom to pull on his own.

Ned and Matt soon followed them out.

"Can we build a fire?" Ned said.

Matt clicked his tongue as he dropped into a chair. "Unfortunately not. Valentina says there's a burn ban."

"Because of the air quality?"

"It's about the wildfire risk. It's been dry as fuck this spring."

"The dark sky will be nice too," Peggy said, pulling a chair closer to the empty fire pit. "The stargazing will be optimal. I checked—there's no moon this weekend."

Once they'd been out for a while, lounging

and talking, Mason realized that his eyes had adapted to the low light. It was amazing how clear the sky was, with the Milky Way plainly visible, spanning the breadth of the sky. Peggy exclaimed when she saw a shooting star, and a while later Ned saw one too.

"That's a satellite," she said, pointing to the sky.

Mason followed the angle of her arm and saw it—a point of light moving slowly through the stars.

"There's three of them together," Matt said, and sure enough, two other nearby points were moving at the same pace, on the same trajectory.

One of them brightened dramatically for a few seconds, then faded back to its original intensity.

"Whoa," Ned said. "What the hell?"

"It's called a satellite flare," Peggy said. "It's when the solar panels catch the sun at just the right angle."

"Even though the sun is below the horizon?" Mason said.

"It is for us, but not for the satellite. Reflected sunlight is the only reason you can see it at all."

"So why are there three of them?" Matt said.

"It's those internet connectivity ones. They keep launching them in fleets, and they travel like that, in series. There's literally thousands of them up there. These three are headed southeast, so they'll disappear when they enter the earth's shadow."

Sure enough, a few moments later, they faded out, one by one.

"How do you know that's southeast?" Mason said, still gazing at the sky.

"How do you not know that's southeast?"

He couldn't see her expression in the darkness, but he knew she'd have one eyebrow raised in mock skepticism.

"I don't happen to have my compass on me."

"Everything west of the Mississippi was platted on a grid," she said, "aligned to the cardinal compass points. The road we drove in on, for example. It runs straight north."

Mason pulled out his phone, wincing at the brightness of the screen, and checked the map of where they were.

"I see it now," he said. "It's totally a grid. Those hills are northeast of us."

"I did a lot of map stuff when I was into geocaching," she said.

He tucked his phone away. "I remember."

"My renaissance woman," Matt said, and reached over to squeeze her arm.

It was true—Peggy tended to focus on a specific art or skill for a few months and then move on to something else. Some had been messy, with plaster and ink and paint left around the kitchen.

He'd been happy to see those over with. Others had a lasting benefit, like her graphic design skills, and knowing random things like the map grid. Personally Mason was glad she'd never abandoned the vegan cooking, and of course her music.

A while later, Ned sat up. "It's getting chilly. I'm going inside to do some reading."

"Too cold for me too." Peggy rose.

"I won't be long," Matt said, and she leaned in to kiss him.

"So how are things going with Peggy?" Mason said, once they were alone.

"Great. I think we've found a groove. We manage to be tolerant of each other. What about you two? You've been together as long as I've known you."

"The only issue we have is that Ned doesn't buy the psychic stuff. But I think I'm at peace with that. We can't share everything."

"Still, it's a big part of your life."

"But not the only part. And because of his twelve-step thing, he doesn't tell me what to do."

"I'm kind of amazed that he doesn't mind us drinking when he can't."

"I think it's more about behavior than about the booze itself. If we got blotto and acted like drunks, that would trigger him. But wine with dinner is no big deal."

"More satellites," Matt said, and pointed to the sky.

Mason watched as the duo of pinpoints moved slowly overhead, in the same arc as the earlier ones, northwest to southeast. Then one of them stopped moving while the other continued on its path.

"Are you sure that's what they are?" he said.

"What the actual fuck?"

"Maybe it's the space brothers."

"I do not need any paranormal bullshit right now."

"It might not be paranormal," Mason said, his gaze focused on the point of light.

"Satellites can't just stop dead like that. They're moving extremely fast."

"Maybe it's an airplane?"

"Planes can't do that either. Plus they always have running lights. Red and green and one that flickers."

"I don't want to look away. I won't be able to find it again."

"It does blend in with the stars. Are we absolutely sure it didn't just fade out right in front of a star? Like an optical illusion."

At that moment the point brightened, like the satellite flare they'd seen earlier, and rather than dimming again it flashed across the sky, a momentary bright streak, like a meteor, and disappeared.

"Fuck me," Matt muttered, and got up. "I do not have time for this."

"What the hell was that?" Mason said. He could feel his skin prickling. "Don't you want to parse it?"

"I don't have any answers, Braithwaite." He stepped toward the kitchen door. "I'm afraid you're on your own."

Mason sat for a while, staring at the sky. Matt had a strained relationship with this stuff sometimes, but it made no sense to act like it hadn't happened.

Was the phenomenon directed at Mason specifically, he wondered, or was it just general weirdness, accessible to everybody? Closing his eyes, he tried to tune in to the hidden part of reality. All he got was the same feeling of high energy, like things were cranked up well beyond the baseline. It was exhilarating, in a way, the sensation that he was floating in a sea of unlimited potential. He gave up on getting anything more specific, and sat back and watched the sky for a while. Not seeing anything else that was eerie or inexplicable, he went inside.

Ned was already in bed, asleep, his novel folded open on his belly. Mason ditched his clothes and set Ned's book on the nightstand, then climbed in beside him and killed the light.

It took a while before he was able to sleep,

thinking about the lights in the sky. Maybe it shouldn't be a surprise, he reasoned. The Southwestern desert was ground zero for UFO sightings and saucer crashes.

Two

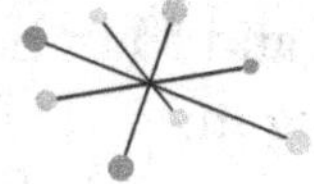

BRIGHT SUNLIGHT STREAMING IN and the smell of java and cooking woke him. Once he'd dressed and washed up, he went out to the kitchen.

"Scrambled tofu," Peggy said, by way of greeting. She was wearing a white kitchen apron, and Ned was beside her, flipping a tortilla in a skillet with a pair of tongs.

"It smells amazing," he said, and poured himself a coffee.

Matt was nearby, at the dining table, with his own mug. "So did the space brothers come down last night?"

"They did," Mason said, eyeing him as he sat across the table, "and they asked about you."

"Some of the early alien visitors were actually hot women," he said. "One I remember reading about specifically is Aura Rhanes. She was a saucer captain, and the guy who met her said she was 'tops in shapeliness and beauty.' I'm not surprised she'd ask for me."

Peggy and Ned brought plates over, scrambled tofu and tortillas and salsa, and sat down with them. Mason and Matt both complimented the food as they dug in.

"I'm not sure whether I should be jealous of a flying-saucer pilot or not," Peggy said, tearing a tortilla in half.

"They used to take earthlings to visit their home planets," Matt said, waving dismissively, "but it was mostly just to show them around. It never took more than an afternoon, and there wasn't much hanky-panky. You have to watch out for the ones in the long pink spaceships, though. They steal."

Mason laughed. "So it wasn't all amity and enlightenment from space?"

"The ones in the pink ships didn't know they were doing anything wrong," Matt said. "If you weren't wearing something, or holding it in your hand, to them it was unowned, and they'd take it. They had very red skin, and hair like pinfeathers, and kind of elongated heads." He gestured with his palm above his own head.

"Did they get into our dryer?" Ned said. "Maybe that's where the missing socks go."

"In 1967 they agreed to stop visiting our planet," Matt said. "Too much stuff was disappearing."

"How do you know all this?" Peggy demanded.

"I read some books by the early contactees. I guess it was part of my own psychic explorations. There are some great titles: *Flying Saucers Have Landed,* and *Aboard a Flying Saucer,* and *I Rode a Flying Saucer.* How could any rational person choose not to read books with names like that?"

Ned chuckled and arched his back. "Even with all the aliens, this is such a great place to spend the weekend."

"Who's up for a hike?" Peggy said. "I want to climb that hill."

"Maybe it's the altitude," Ned said, "but I'm not feeling especially energetic today. I'm just going to chill."

Matt waved his fork. "I'll go with you."

After they'd eaten, Mason volunteered to clean up. Matt and Peggy walked off into the landscape, and Ned took his novel outside. Later, when Mason stepped out, he found Ned reclining in a sun lounger, dark glasses on, absorbed in his book.

"I can't believe you can just sit in direct sunlight like that," Mason said.

"It feels good. I'll move into the shade later."

"I feel like a vampire by comparison."

"It's your redheaded complexion. It evolved for places like the Hebrides or Shetland, where it's overcast forty days a month. My skin, on the other hand, was built for sunny Tenochtitlan."

"I guess I should have brought a hat."

"Check it out—you can see them on the hill," Ned said, gesturing toward the horizon.

When he looked, he could see two figures in the distance, Matt's white shirt and Peggy's blue backpack, inching slowly along the double track that wound up the hillside.

Mason stepped over to the hammock suspended from the house's eaves. "I didn't notice this last night."

"I tried it, but it's too cool for me out of the sun."

"Shade is just what I need. I'm going to grab a book," he said, and went back inside.

There was a low bookstand in the corner near the sofa, and he knelt in front of it, cocking his head to read the spines. There were some romance novels, and mysteries, and a couple of weathered biology textbooks, but Mason pulled out a volume titled *Homesteaders, Marines, and Space Aliens: The Morongo Basin in the Twentieth*

Century. He didn't even need to read the inside flap—this was definitely the book for today.

Once he'd climbed into the hammock and got comfortable, he started to leaf through the contents. The most interesting chapters were about Giant Rock, an oversize boulder on public land just a few miles from here. Starting in the early 1950s, the guy who ran the airstrip adjacent to the rock hosted flying-saucer events several times a year. They sounded like free-for-all countercultural meet-ups, and the host channeled messages from the space brothers, who were hovering out of sight in saucers far overhead.

It took effort to get out here back then, and people came for the speakers and to network with other saucer-heads. You had to bring your own food, but people camped out and had fun with it. More chillingly, the FBI kept a clandestine sharp eye on the events, suspicious that something so far outside the mainstream might be run by subversives.

The book contained a sampling of the messages transmitted from the space brothers. They wanted earthlings to live in peace, and give up atomic weapons, and change their destructive ways before it was too late. It made sense that the feds would be interested in that—any call for peace and disarmament in that paranoid era would easily be mistaken for commie propaganda.

Flipping the page, he found a brief story about a woman who was headed to one of the saucer meet-ups, but never made it. On the way she got lost in the desert, her car stuck in the sand. She walked to an empty homesteader cabin, and broke in, but there was no water there, and before she could make it back to her car, she died of dehydration and exposure. She was a journalist from Los Angeles, and her plan had been to write about the saucer event.

Setting the book down, Mason stared out at the landscape, at the hill Peggy and Matt were climbing. They weren't in view anymore. The land seemed innocuous right now, and placid, even inviting. But this really was an extreme climate, an unforgiving place if you weren't prepared for it.

The book named her as Geraldine Reed. Mason pulled out his phone and did a web search, squinting to see the screen in the bright daylight. There were a couple of newspaper stories about her death, both dated 1953. One of the articles explained that she'd left her cat, Sylvester, with a friend in Los Angeles the day before she drove out to the Mojave. The friend said Sylvester knew when his human had died, as he started yowling inconsolably. A grainy black-and-white photo revealed Sylvester to be black with luminous eyes, and Geraldine's friend to be an austere woman with sharp cheekbones, her gray hair piled on her head.

A while later Peggy and Matt walked into the yard, and Mason looked up from his reading to greet them.

"How was the hike?"

Peggy put a finger to her lips and pointed to Ned, sleeping in the sun, his book facedown on his chest.

"It's beautiful here," she said, her voice low. "Those hills aren't hard to climb."

"The ground is rocky, though," Matt said, pulling off his hat. "You need sturdy shoes."

"The hammock looks comfy," Peggy said. "What are you reading?"

"It's about a psychic cat."

"You should totally get one of those," Matt said.

Peggy pulled off her backpack. "No way. We don't have room for a litter box." She pushed a wisp of hair behind her ear. "We decided we're going to make pancakes, if you're interested. Once I've drunk all the water."

"I won't lie to you, Peggy," Mason said, holding her gaze. "I have to say I'm extremely interested."

A while later she stepped outside to summon the two of them in, rousing Ned from his nap. After they'd eaten, Ned started to clean up.

"I want to be outside," Peggy said, and she and Matt went out into the afternoon sun.

Near the front door there was a broad-brimmed straw hat hanging on a hook, and Mason tried it on. Of course it was too small for him, and sat awkwardly on the crown of his head, but it would keep the sun off, and he stepped outside and sat with Matt and Peggy around the empty fire pit.

"New hat?" Peggy said. "I love the flowered band."

Mason pulled it off for a moment to check. A wide ribbon of pastel-colored blossoms ran around it, just above the brim.

"I hadn't noticed that. I think it belongs to Valentina." He set it back on his head. "What's the view like up on that hill?"

"You can see the flats from the top," Peggy said. "They're on the far side. It looks pretty lifeless compared to here. There aren't any Joshua trees, just the creosotes. Even so, it's absolutely beautiful."

"Why are there so many Joshua trees here but not over there?"

"It's at lower elevation," Matt said. "Joshua trees grow in pretty limited conditions. Technically they're endangered."

"So what does the desert mean?" Mason said.

Matt chuckled. "I'm a scientist, not a philosopher, Braithwaite."

"Still, you must get a vibe."

"Open space, maybe?" he said. "Isolation?"

"That's what it is, but what do those things mean?"

"That sounds like a metaphysical question," Peggy said. "What does it mean to you?"

"You sound like my shrink," Mason said flatly. "I'm not sure. Maybe something about resilience, or tenacity."

"This place definitely symbolizes those ideas, sure."

Matt waved an arm. "In addition, I can assure you that everything here is willing to kill you."

Mason laughed. "What do you mean?"

"Every plant has thorns or spines. Even that bush that looks all green and soft. I think it's an *Acacia*. They bite you if you touch them."

"He's right," Peggy said. "When the wind died down out there, we met the most persistent flies I've ever seen."

"Valentina says that about the people too," Matt said. "Persistent, and rugged, with a crusty veneer."

"They're desert rats," Mason said.

"I'm sure not all of them are, but generally I'd say that rings true."

"Are you wearing sunblock?" Peggy said, her brow furrowing. "That hat doesn't cover everything, and you look a little pink."

"That's the only color I can muster besides

pasty. I guess I should be in the shade."

He moved back to the hammock, and dug into the history book again, rereading the pages about Geraldine. It seemed so tragic, her death so pointless. Eventually Matt and Peggy went inside, and as the sun sank low in the sky, he took a nap. A while later Ned stepped outside.

"It's nice out here now," he said.

"It's been nice all day."

"Dinner's ready. We made barley pilaf."

"You just whipped that up, in someone else's kitchen?"

Ned chuckled. "It's not that difficult."

Over dinner they talked about Peggy and Matt's walk in the hills, and the views, and the landscape. Moving her empty plate away, Peggy reached for the history book, sitting at the end of the table.

"Is this what you were reading?" she said. "What part of local history involves a psychic cat?"

"In 1953 this writer drove out from LA to interview the Giant Rock people about the space brothers. Her name was Geraldine. She got lost, and her car got stuck in the sand. I think it was somewhere east of here, maybe on the flats, where the base is now. She died of exposure."

Peggy frowned. "That's horrible."

"How does the psychic cat play into it?" Ned said.

"Geraldine left her cat with a friend in the city. Sylvester knew exactly when she died."

"I bet Sylvester was a black cat."

Mason eyed him. "How did you know that?"

"I know how your world works."

"It sounds like she was unprepared for the desert," Matt said.

"She'd made several trips to Giant Rock before, but never alone. There was no GPS back then."

"Even today, though, nature can be tough," Ned said. "The desert is uninhabited for a reason. You have to be prepared to survive out here."

Mason waved a hand. "You're just saying that because the internet's poky and you can't get food delivered."

❦

THE FOUR OF THEM sat outside again after dark, watching the sky. Eventually Peggy and Matt went in.

"It's getting cold," Ned said, and stepped over to Mason's chair, climbing onto his lap, looping his arm behind Mason's neck.

"You're nice and warm."

Ned kissed his neck, then met his mouth, and they spent a minute in it. Mason relished the warmth and the proximity.

"Hold up," Ned said, pulling away, craning to

look out across the landscape.

Mason followed his gaze into the blackness, toward the road, and then saw it too. A pale blue light, slowly drifting sideways along the ground.

"Are you seeing that?"

"It looks like an orb."

"Maybe it's a flashlight," Ned said. "Someone's walking up the road, or through the countryside."

"It's too steady. When someone's walking, the light bounces around. That thing is floating. It also doesn't look like a flashlight to me. It looks like a sphere."

Ned stood up. "Let's go see."

"Should I get a flashlight?"

"I can see well enough by starlight not to trip."

"I guess my eyes are adjusted to the dark too."

As they walked around the house and out onto the road, another orb appeared. Both were off in the landscape, among the creosote bushes and the Joshua trees, nowhere near the roadway. It was hard to tell how far away they were, or how large they were, drifting leisurely above the ground.

At the same moment both orbs changed color, from pale blue to soft orange, and a moment later both winked off, then simultaneously winked on again.

Ned stopped walking. "I know what you're thinking. Do not say it."

"How do you know what I'm thinking? Are you the psychic now?"

"You're going to say those things are paranormal, and we've entered woo-woo land."

Mason stifled a retort. "You have to admit they look pretty freaking weird. Do you have an explanation?"

Ned didn't answer, and they stood in silence, watching the orbs. One of them was larger now. Maybe it had drifted closer to them, or maybe it had swollen in size. Then, farther down the road, two round yellow lights appeared, as if cresting a rise. A sharp inhale of breath told him Ned saw them too.

"Valentina's is the only house on this road," Ned said. "Who's driving up here at this hour?"

"Those don't look like headlights. They're not bright enough."

"Of course they're headlights."

As they watched, the pair rose a little higher, as if getting closer, and then started to drift sideways, toward the orbs.

"Oh, man," Ned said, under his breath.

"You know about cars. Do you know any vehicle that can drive sideways?"

"That would be no."

"They're higher than the foliage. I can see the tops of the bushes illuminated below."

"That means at least eight feet up."

The lights rose a little as they drifted toward the orbs, and then all the lights winked out at once. He and Ned stood in silence for a moment, waiting, watching the dark landscape.

"Maybe the show's over," Mason said finally.

"There has to be a rational explanation for this."

As Ned finished the sentence, a brilliant white light shone from directly above him, a spotlight aimed down at him, turning night into day. Ned froze, and then shielded his eyes, and tried to look up.

Mason stood rooted to the ground, a few feet away, wincing at the brightness, the blood pounding in his ears. The source of the blinding glare seemed to be a few feet over Ned's head, but even squinting, he couldn't make out where it was coming from. He could see every hair on his head in sharp detail.

The light winked off again a moment later. Mason's night vision was blown now, and he stood there blinking in the total darkness, breathing hard from the rush of adrenaline. He heard Ned's footsteps on the dirt road, walking away, toward the house.

"Hold up," Mason said. "Are you OK?"

Ned didn't answer, and Mason caught up to him, briefly touching his shoulder as they walked abreast. The only point of reference they had was the faint light in the windows of the house in the distance. Finally Ned spoke, his tone intent.

"What the hell was that?"

"I don't know, but it definitely wasn't part of baseline reality."

"At least you're not trying to tell me it was aliens."

"It could be."

"There's lots of other things it could be that are more likely than aliens," Ned said.

"Like what?"

"Some new military technology they're testing."

"Why would they do that on Valentina's land when the biggest marine base in the country is right over that hill?"

"Maybe it went off course."

Mason stifled a sigh. "Or maybe it was something bleeding through from the unseen part of reality."

Back in the house, they got ready for bed, treading quietly because Matt and Peggy had already retired. Ned went to have a shower, and Mason climbed under the covers and plugged in his phone. He heard the water running as he lay there, thinking about what they'd seen. Ned was gone for a long time, and when he finally came to bed, he climbed on top of Mason and leaned in to meet his mouth.

As Ned pulled back, Mason ran a hand into his hair. "Has the paranormal stuff got you wound up?"

"It's all about you. So unafraid, running toward the weird lights and the floating RV instead of away from it. You were waiting for another spotlight. I bet you were hoping it would zap you too."

"Why do you say it was an RV?"

"The lights were set fairly far apart," Ned said. "It looked like the front end of an RV."

"I'd call that a psychic insight."

Ned caressed his chest. "We'll have to be quiet. Granny's cabin has thin walls."

Three

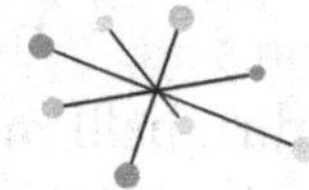

IN THE MORNING, AFTER they'd eaten and Mason was sufficiently caffeinated, when they were all still sitting at the dining table, Matt spoke.

"Who's up for a trip to Giant Rock? I want to see where the saucer meetings were held. It's just a few miles from here."

"Definitely," Mason said. "I'm in."

"I'm thinking it's more of a hammock type day for me," Ned said. "But take the Crown Vic." He dug in his pocket and set the car keys on the table.

"Not a touring day for me either," Peggy said.

"That sounds more like an outing for the psychic boys."

"You people have no freaking imagination," Matt muttered, and scooped up the keys.

"Don't slow down when you hit that sandy patch on the road," Ned said. "You'll get stuck."

Mason grabbed Valentina's ill-fitting straw hat from beside the door as they walked out, and Matt climbed behind the wheel of the Crown Vic, taking a minute to adjust the seat and the mirrors.

"Go easy," Mason said. "If Ned hears his tires peeling out on the dirt, he'll make you clean the whole car with a toothbrush."

Matt navigated to the paved road, successfully traversing the sandy patch. Giant Rock was farther than he'd estimated, first on the pavement, and then a dusty desert track for the last few miles. The landscape here was lower than at Valentina's place, and much flatter, and devoid of the striking spiky Joshua trees. Standing at the edge of a rocky hill and facing a flat expanse of desert, the giant boulder loomed large as they drove up on it. A dozen vehicles and tents were parked at its base.

"That's where the runway was," Matt said, pointing out the salt pan on the flats.

"What are all these people doing here?"

"It's public land, but it's not protected, like a national park is."

"So it's a free-for-all." Mason grabbed the flowery straw hat and popped his door handle.

"It looks more like a goddamn homeless encampment."

They climbed out and walked toward the boulder, giving the tents a wide berth.

"I bet it wasn't covered with graffiti in the 1950s," Mason said.

"What a fucking mess."

"This part that broke off is white inside. The split looks new."

"In geological terms, it is," Matt said. "That happened in 2000. Right after the turn of the millennium. Of course some New Agers took credit for it. The more likely explanation is that it split because people had been building bonfires under that overhang for decades."

They walked across a dusty concrete pad, its rectangular shape implying that it might have once hosted a structure, and circumnavigated the rock. In a shady spot behind it, a small group of people sat in a circle, around a blackened patch of earth that at some point must have been a campfire. Several of them had cans of beer in hand.

"How are you doing?" Matt said, and Mason greeted them too as they passed by.

"I love your hat," one of them said.

Mason didn't respond to that, but he could feel his face heating up.

On the other side of the rock Matt pointed out an oblong patch of earth.

"This is where the first guy who lived here dug an underground bunker. He actually lived under the rock. So did the guy who hosted the saucer meet-ups. They filled it in after he left."

"You know all this from those early contactee books?"

"That, and I did some cramming about Giant Rock in anticipation of this weekend." He looked up at the rock, then surveyed the graffiti. "I have to admit I'm a little disappointed."

"Maybe that's why the rock split. It was depressed about its declining fortunes."

Matt chuckled. "By the turn of the millennium it had no fucks left to give. It just gave up."

From somewhere among the tents came the sound of glass breaking, and then a muffled angry voice.

"We can go," Matt said, and they walked back to the Crown Vic.

Once they were cruising on the dirt track, Mason said, "Things change all the time. Maybe the site will get protected status someday, and the feds will clean it up."

"It doesn't fucking matter to me. I just wanted to see it."

But Mason could tell that his mood had changed, that he'd grown somber. He could see that it was a little depressing—there were lots of neglected ruins around the Mojave and up in the Sierra, old mines and abandoned homesteads and ghost towns, but they weren't usually so visibly abused.

When they got back to the house, Peggy was lounging in the hammock, and Ned was in one of the chairs around the fire pit.

"How was Giant Rock?" Ned said, setting down his book.

Matt scoffed. "Trashed. You didn't miss anything."

"You mean there's garbage dumped around it?" Peggy said.

"It's thoroughly graffitied. It looks like those fucked-up rail yards along the LA River. Complete with a homeless encampment."

"I definitely want to get out into the natural landscape after that," Mason said. "Was there graffiti on your hike yesterday?"

"Nothing like that," Peggy said. "Just walk toward the hill. There's a jeep trail leading up, so it's not pristine, but the trail makes the hiking easy. We didn't see another person the whole time."

Once he'd gone inside and drunk a few glasses of water, Mason put on Valentina's ill-fitting straw hat again, and pulled on his sunglasses, and walked toward the hill. He found the base of the jeep trail, leading up from the sandy flatland onto the rocky hillside, and as promised, the land bore no other trace of human activity.

On the way up he stopped to look over the landscape, to the distant boulder-strewn mountains and the homesteads between. Thinking about last night, it was hard to intuit what those orbs and the RV really were, even when he cleared his mind and sought insight. Even labeling them as "orbs" and "RV" was detrimental—the words forced the phenomena into a box, and that hobbled any further understanding. He knew that with the unexplained, sometimes certainty was a trap.

Up ahead on the double track he saw movement, and stopped to look. A coyote stepped onto the trail, just a little higher on the hillside. It paused and looked at Mason, panting, its tongue lolling like a dog's. But something was off—it was too big. In the city, coyotes were the size of a skinny pit bull or smaller, and this thing was much larger, bigger than a shepherd or a Doberman.

It turned away and kept walking, picking its way through the rocks and brush. The color was wrong too—too gray, almost bluish-gray, like gunmetal. Coyotes were usually dark brown. As the creature sauntered out of view, behind some rocks and down into a wash, Mason felt the hair on his neck stand up with the realization that maybe it wasn't a coyote at all. He'd come across a *nagual* before, a guy who could shapeshift into animal form.

"Come and talk to me, if you want," Mason called, just loud enough that the creature would hear him.

No reply came, and he started to feel a little foolish. Not everything was paranormal. Maybe it was just a big coyote. With a deep breath he continued up the hill.

Once he was at the top, he saw that Peggy hadn't overstated it—there was an excellent view of the flats. It was all military land, he knew, but he couldn't see any evidence of the base, except some structures far away in the haze, at the foot of the distant mountains. It looked drier than here, as there was much less plant life, and in the distance, at the lowest point, he could make out the white oval of a salt pan.

Somewhere out there is where Geraldine succumbed, stuck in the sand. She didn't know what Ned knew—you had to speed through it not to get stuck. And why hadn't she taken water with her?

Facing the vast flat expanse, he sat on the ground and closed his eyes, trying to shift into a parallel state of perception, waiting for psychic insight. What came to him wasn't clear-cut information, just a feeling of saturation, the colors of this place, the dark green flora and pink and tan earth that surrounded him, the white quartz and black gneiss. The insight was sharper, the colors more vivid than what he'd been looking at with his regular senses—more immediate, more energized.

Eventually he opened his eyes. The saucerheads had thought this place was different, that it had some kind of earth energy that attracted the space brothers, and he could definitely feel it. There was more to it than Ned's pronouncement that it was just dry air.

Under his breath, he spoke aloud. "What happened to you, Geraldine?"

Following the double track, he made his way back down the hill, soon walking up on the house. In the kitchen he downed a glass of water, then another, and ditched Valentina's hat before he joined Matt and Peggy in the backyard. It was warmer today, and Ned was dozing in the hammock.

"Are the coyotes out here a different species than in town?" Mason said, dropping into one of the chairs at the fire pit. He leaned down to loosen his shoelaces.

"I don't know for sure," Matt said, "but I seriously doubt it."

"I saw one on the hill that seemed really big."

"They might have a healthier diet in the

natural environment. Rodents and rabbits instead of leftover sheet cake and french fries, like in LA."

"So I've been thinking more about Geraldine."

"And psychic Sylvester?" Peggy said. "I don't think we need a cat."

"Not about the cat. About what happened to her. If you get some distance from the details, and think about it from farther away, what does it mean?"

Matt frowned. "She was on a quest for knowledge, right? That's a universal theme. But then there's the fucked-up twist to it, her tragic ending."

"Maybe Geraldine is symbolic of a quest in general," Peggy said. "Like in literature."

"We're not used to that kind of story, though," Matt said. "In fiction the hero usually prevails."

"In this case, the heroine," she said, eyeing him. "And not always. Pre-American literature was way less optimistic. Gilgamesh got burned, like Geraldine did."

Mason cocked his head. "Who was Gilgamesh?"

"A Mesopotamian hero. Basically his story is a cautionary tale about the pursuit of glory."

"I love that you know that."

"Remember when I was learning to write cuneiform?"

"How could I forget? There were clay tablets

all over the house for weeks."

"You actually used clay to practice cuneiform?" Matt said, grinning at her.

She waved dismissively. "It was modeling clay. I wasn't going to practice a five-thousand-year-old script with a ballpoint. To learn it properly you have to press a stick into wet clay."

"I don't know if Geraldine was intent on attaining glory," Mason said. "She just wanted to write about the saucer-heads."

Matt shifted in his chair. "Maybe that's why it resonates with you."

"Meaning what?"

"She was a researcher, like you are. Intent on digging into a paranormal mystery, like you do."

"At the cost of her life," Peggy said quietly.

"Standing on that hill," Mason said, "looking out at the flatlands, I get how you could get lost there."

"Maybe that's what the desert represents," Peggy said. "An expansive place to lose yourself."

Mason nodded. "You know, Geraldine made her last trip out here in the summer of 1953. I've spent time in 1952 more than once."

"You want to go back and save her?" Peggy said.

"I'm not sure that's possible. It just feels like she's someone who should have had a chance to complete her research. Her demise feels wrong.

48

Like it was a pointless mistake."

"You can change the past," Matt said, "but it changes the present. You know that. The boss cautions us about it every time we help her out. 'Don't change anything,' she says."

He was talking about Hanh, ostensibly a nail salon owner back in the city who had some role in the liminal world, either as a gatekeeper or a guardian. She'd saved Mason's neck once, and Matt's too on a separate occasion, and since then she sometimes asked for their help with paranormal work.

"I've read the theory that if you change something in the past, reality rearranges itself to achieve the same outcome," Peggy said. "So if you stop Geraldine from getting stuck in the sand, maybe she'll get killed in a crash ten minutes later."

"I don't think it works that way," Matt said, sitting up in his chair. "It's more like when you change something, your timeline diverges."

"So there are two alternate realities?"

"I bet it's a lot more than two. They bifurcate when things change and blend again when conditions converge in some other way."

"How does it work, exactly, when you bleed through?" she said.

"I can't explain the mechanism," Mason said. "The way I understand it is that my subconscious mind sidesteps the official version of reality that we all agree on."

"So anyone could do it."

"Sure, with enough energy. I can't go very far without help, and I definitely can't take my body very far."

"Isn't it more about a step backward than a step sideways?" she said. "My perception of time is that it's linear."

"Everything exists all at once," Matt said. "That woman and her cat exist now, alternately with our present, just as vividly as we do. The linear thing is just how your conscious mind has learned to organize it."

Peggy sighed. "It's so hard to conceptualize."

"It just feels like I can't sit on my hands," Mason said. "I know I can change things for the better."

"Personally I don't think it's a great idea," Matt said. "I've been struggling with this stuff lately."

"Psychic stuff?"

"I have enough trouble navigating the superficial version of the world, you know? Adding this infinite unseen reality is a lot to deal with. Sometimes I wish I could just tune it out."

Mason nodded. "I think that's what most people do."

"It's tough out there for a tenured professor,"

Peggy said, raising her eyebrows. "With your housing allowance and staff budget and all."

"You know what I mean. It's not about material hardship. It's about knowing too much."

"I wondered why you avoided that anomalous stuff the other night," Mason said. "It sucks for me that you don't want to deal—I don't have many psychic peers that I can commiserate with."

Peggy frowned. "What anomalous stuff?"

Mason gestured vaguely. "Just some lights in the sky."

"Explain," she said flatly.

"I can describe it, but I can't explain it," Mason said, and told her what they'd seen.

"Anyway," Matt said, his tone pointed, "if you do this, if you bleed through to Geraldine's time, make sure you consider all the possible outcomes."

"Ultimately it'll be up to Hanh. She's the only one who can get me there."

"Changing someone's destiny sounds really irresponsible," Peggy said. "You're not a deity."

"Neither was the guy who invented the polio vaccine, but think of how many people's lives he saved. I just want to fix the one."

"'Fix' her life?" She waggled her fingers to put air quotes around the word. "You sound like an egomaniac."

"What if she survives and then she starts a UFO cult?" Matt said. "There were a few of those around, back in the day."

"Or what if you save her," Peggy said, "and then with her extended time she invents a black hole device that crushes the entire planet—before you're even born?" She mimed crumpling paper into a ball.

Mason frowned. "She's a newspaper woman, not a religious nut, and not a mad scientist."

"*Was*, Mason." Peggy threw up her hands. "Not 'is.'"

Matt chuckled. "You're already there with her in your head."

Peggy leaned toward him. "I'm just saying—and this is something I tell my students—you need to check yourself before you wreck yourself."

"I'll keep that in mind."

She glanced at the hammock. "And don't tell Ned. He'll add it to the list of evidence that you're losing touch with reality."

AFTER ANOTHER LIGHT MEAL, as the sun got low in the sky, they packed up the kitchen and loaded their bags into the car, working quietly, subdued at the thought of heading back to regular life.

"Good-bye, house," Peggy said, as they pulled away.

Once Ned had driven through the sandy stretch on the dirt road, and turned onto the pavement, she spoke again.

"I wish we'd done this next weekend, so we could stay longer. It's spring break."

"We'll come back," Matt said. "I'll bug Valentina to let us use it again. Maybe we'll trade time here for some of your amazing cooking."

The drive back to LA was mostly quiet, and calm because of Ned's relaxed attentive driving. The sun disappeared as they dropped through the Gorgonio Pass, and the sky grew dark. Mason knew how they all felt, comfortable and contented and exhausted from the sun and the exercise.

Four

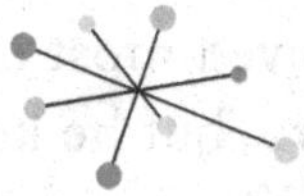

Waking on Monday morning, in the familiar comfort of his own bed, Mason tried to hold on to the wisps of the dream world. There had been airplanes, he remembered, little ones, lined up in a row. Walking between them, he was carrying something. He couldn't remember what it was, but his hands were full, and it was heavy.

Ned was in his office, he saw as he walked by on his way to the kitchen, and he stuck his head in to say hello. Ned worked on something to do with mortgages, from home most of the time, although he went out for meetings now and then with his bankers and his clients.

Bleary-eyed, Mason struggled to get the espresso machine working, pressing the coffee into the filter, then dumped the little pot of steaming life into a mug and sat at the kitchen counter. Once a sufficient quantity of caffeine was coursing through his veins, he ate some muesli and an apple, resisting the urge to brew a second pot of java. He didn't want to be too alert today—there was low-key work to do.

Mason had moved most of his work stuff to his office downtown, but he kept some books on the shelves in Ned's office, where his desk had once been. Ned was absorbed in his computer screen when he stepped in, but he murmured a greeting. Mason found the book he wanted: *Beyond the Dial.* It was about psychic information that came through off-channel audio and video recordings, and it contained a specific technique he wanted to try.

Standing at the bookcase, he flipped through the text, and found the relevant page, and read through it. No way was he going to do this here, he decided, glancing at Ned. He'd go to his own office. Once he was dressed, in chinos and a long-sleeved shirt for the cool weather, and he'd tucked the book into his backpack, he went back to Ned's desk to tell him he was headed out.

In the garage he fastened the velcro strap

around his ankle to keep his pant leg out of his bicycle chain, then wheeled his steed outside and coasted down the hill. The chilly winter air felt good, ruffling his hair as he cycled toward the boulevard, leaning into the curves. Minutes later he pulled up at the metro station and carried his wheels down the steps.

Standing with his bicycle at the end of the car, he rode downtown and changed trains, then disembarked at the stop in Lincoln Heights where the giant thrift store was. He locked his wheels to the bike rack out front and walked into the cavernous space, ogling the clothes racks but resisting the urge to stop and paw through them, instead heading into the electronics room.

He knew he'd find the component he needed, and soon he'd located a whole shelf of them—a dozen old VCRs. Picking up the most compact of the options, he saw that it had a strip of masking tape on top, with FUNCIONA written on it in black marker. Mason didn't speak the language, but even with his taco-cart Spanish he knew that meant the device was in working order. The price tag said $25, so he tucked it under his arm, then grabbed a couple of video cables to go with it.

A videotape was part of the deal, he remembered, eyeing a nearby bin full of them. None of these were new, but it wouldn't matter—he could record over whatever was on it. He took one that looked lightly used and headed toward the register.

As he set the machine on the counter, he flashed the clerk a smile. "Can I get all this for twenty?"

She furrowed her brow and peeled the price tag off the machine. "How about everything for twenty-five?"

Mason paid her and squatted on the concrete floor for a moment to stuff the machine into his backpack, then went out to unlock his bicycle, and headed back to the metro.

Soon he was carrying his wheels up out of the ground across from his office building. It always lifted his spirits to see it, with its soaring lines, the beautiful pink terra-cotta tile of its facade. The structure dated to the art deco era, and he'd been around it long enough to know some of its secrets.

As he strode into the ornate lobby, the guard on the front desk, a chubby guy in a dark-blue uniform, glanced up and greeted him.

"Mr. Braithwaite."

"It's just Mason," he said, and smiled.

"Not all the tenants are so casual. Better safe than sorry."

He kicked down his bike stand outside the mail room while he ducked in to check his box. The elevators had been restored to their erstwhile glory, the rich mahogany wall panels and an antique floor indicator, with a brass needle that swung from number to number. Mason wheeled his bicycle inside and pressed the button for 10.

Unlike the lobby, the offices upstairs hadn't been restored but rather renovated in spare modern style, with open concrete floors and ceilings. His space was mostly one big room, with tall windows that looked out at the towers of the Financial District. A washroom and storage space were at the back, and thrift-store lounge furniture sat under the windows, with his desk facing them.

He parked his bicycle in the open space near his conference table. It was circular so that he could use it for séances, but beneath the black cloth it was just an old dining table that he'd bought at the thrift store.

Next to the sofa he set the VCR on the floor and then found a socket to plug it in. The indicator lights came on, and it made a soft mechanical whirring sound. Hopefully that meant it was working—he wasn't going to plug it into a TV, not yet. Sliding the videotape out of its sleeve, he pushed it into the machine and spent a minute figuring out how to make it record.

Thumbing through *Beyond the Dial* to reread the exercise, he found that the author suggested staying awake for twenty-four hours before trying it, so that your dreams would be twice as strong. Mason was already psychic, he reasoned, so he had a head start—he could skip the pain of an all-nighter.

Over at his desk, he found a box cutter in the drawer and used it to cut the end off one of the video cables, then stripped the end of the wire bare. From the storage closet he retrieved his fluffy pillow and dropped it on the end of the sofa, then checked the exercise instructions again, and plugged the video cable into the input socket on the VCR. Stepping to his desk again to retrieve a roll of masking tape, he ripped off a piece, and stretched out on the sofa, then taped the bare wire at the end of the video cable to the spot between his eyebrows.

The author said that just laying your head near the VCR would work, but logically the wire to the third eye provided a stronger connection. Fiddling with the buttons on the machine, he set it to tape for three hours, then pressed the button marked RECORD.

With the wire draped over the armrest, he shifted on the sofa to get comfortable. He hadn't had that much coffee today, and none in the last hour or so, so it didn't take long to drift off.

SOMETIME LATER MASON WOKE to the sound of the office door opening. The sky outside had faded to the gray of twilight. Lifting his head, he saw Ned stepping in.

"Sorry to wake you," Ned said. As he got closer, his eyes narrowed. "Why is there a wire taped to your forehead?"

"It's a psychic insight thing." Mason sat up and peeled off the masking tape.

"I thought psychics didn't need technology. Doesn't psychic insight come from a direction you can't point to?"

"What are you doing here?" Mason said, standing up to stretch his back.

"I had a meeting downtown. I thought I'd swing by and offer you a ride. We should eat out before Peggy's thing."

"I forgot that was tonight."

"So did I. Luckily my calendar sent me an alert."

Mason knelt beside the VCR and switched it off.

"No judgment," Ned said, "but just so that I understand what I'm seeing, your forehead was plugged into a video recorder."

"My third eye, specifically. The concept is that dreams will leave some imprint in the static on the videotape. Extrasensory information gets encoded in the snow."

"Of course it would." Ned nodded. "I mean, the input wire was taped to your face."

"I know you're being sarcastic," Mason said, straightening up. "It doesn't matter. It's just an experiment—I'm not sure yet whether I can get it to work."

Ned put his hands on his hips. "Oh, I can tell you exactly how well it's going to work."

"What time is it, anyway?"

"It's after five."

"I was out for a while. I must have filled the whole tape. We should go, right? I'll have to watch it later."

"How about that burger joint with the rings?"

Mason wheeled his bicycle into the hallway, and Ned locked the office door, and they rode down to the parking garage. The Crown Vic was waiting at the valet stand. Ned palmed a fin and deftly passed it to the attendant as he took the keys, and thanked him in Spanish, using the guy's name.

It was interesting to watch, Mason thought, lifting his bicycle into the trunk. It wasn't part of his own world—he didn't have a car. It wasn't like Ned to trust one of his babies with anyone, but there was usually nowhere to park around here, and as a tenant Mason had access to the valet. Five bucks seemed like an excessive tip, but maybe that bought extra care for his wheels.

Ned twisted the key in the ignition and popped it into gear, then nosed into the street.

"So why are you using technology instead of your usual meditation thing?"

"I read about the technique in a book, and thought I'd give it a try."

"It looked painful."

"Sometimes you have to suffer a little to get to deeper truths."

Ned scoffed. "Is it for a case?"

"I've been thinking about Geraldine. The woman who got lost in the desert."

"The one with the psychic cat."

"His name was Sylvester. I wanted to get insight into her."

"If Sylvester was psychic, maybe he'll tell you something in the snow on the VCR tape."

"I never thought of that," Mason said, gazing out the window at the dark streets. "I wonder what a projection from a cat would be like?"

"You know I was joking, right?" Ned said, and pulled in at a meter.

The eatery Ned had mentioned was a bar, just up the block, and they went in and found a booth. The attraction was the vegan burgers and fast food. Ned didn't seem to mind being in a pub, but even so, he sat on the side with a view of the front window rather than the bar.

After they'd eaten, they got in the Crown Vic, and Ned headed for the freeway. Peggy was playing at a night market in San Gabriel, a few minutes' drive east. It took a while to get parked in the crowded lot, but soon they were walking among the stalls, laden with fried food and redolent of Southeast Asian spices.

"We could have waited to eat here," Mason said.

"There's nothing vegan. It's a shame, because there's so damn much food."

Toward the back they found the stage, a platform with a curtain behind it and a few rows of benches set up in front. A dozen people were scattered around the space, but most weren't paying attention to the performer on the little stage, instead talking with their friends. Some even had their backs turned. Matt was here, Mason saw, as they walked up near the front. Wearing a dark jacket for the evening air, he sat alone on a bench. As they sat down with him, they exchanged quiet greetings.

There was no amplification, and just a few wan stage lights, but the music was easy to hear. The performer, a stocky guy in a black turtleneck, was playing a violin, and the melody felt sad. It wasn't classical music, Mason decided, watching him play. It was formal but modern. Eventually he finished, and took a little bow to a smattering of applause. Matt clapped loudly and Ned whistled through his fingers. The performer glanced at them and flashed a wry smile.

After he'd walked off, Peggy strode onto the stage, carrying her guitar by its neck, decked out as her Peggy Pregnant persona: a flowered headband over her long straight hair, bell-bottom jeans, and wedges, but most strikingly, a massive faux baby bump under a billowy blouse.

Mason had to laugh—it was always so dissonant to see her wearing that thing. She'd bought it at a studio prop sale, and had created the character Peggy Pregnant around it. There were regular fans who came to her shows, and none of them ever asked why she'd been nine months' pregnant for years on end.

None of the regulars appeared to be here tonight, though, except Matt, and he and Ned tried to compensate by cupping their hands and crying "woo-hoo" as loud as they could.

"Thank you," Peggy said, and surveyed the space, a smile on her face, as if waiting for the nonexistent applause to die down. "Thank you so much." She massaged her belly and winced. "Ooh, this one is kicking."

More of the people lounging on the benches had tuned in, and Mason saw a guy swing his legs around to watch.

Peggy pulled her guitar strap onto her neck, making it look like a laborious process, as if she barely had the strength. When she began to strum the instrument, though, the sound was clear, and the melody bright. After a short lead-in, she began to sing:

I've been waiting for a while now, baby
For you to come and rescue me
Let me play on your side
Maybe your love will set me free

The song had a few verses, and when she finished, the three of them clapped and hooted wildly. A few other spectators joined them.

"Peggy wrote that?" Mason said, leaning toward Matt.

"It's totally hers."

The next song wasn't one of her own. Mason recognized it as an old pop song, "Beautiful People," but they clapped for it just as energetically.

"Just one more," Peggy said, and massaged her belly. "The little one is being rambunctious. He's rocking out to the music. I need to get him a shot of tequila." With no audible reaction, she paused for a moment. "I'm just joking," she said, eyeing the sparse crowd. "He prefers Everclear."

Shifting her guitar, she launched into another song.

Matt leaned in. "This is a cover too."

Mason didn't know the tune, but the lyrics weren't typical of Peggy's own writing, and spoke of kisses and sweet dreams.

When she'd finished, they clapped and hooted, and Peggy took a little bow, then strode off the stage, waving triumphantly.

"Do you want to come backstage?" Matt asked them.

"I want to get out of here," Ned said. "The smell of grilled meat in the air is starting to gross me out. We'll congratulate her at home."

They made their way back to the parking lot, and as they climbed into the Crown Vic, Mason saw that he had a voice mail on his phone. It was from Harmony, a friend who worked at the library.

"I found a picture of you in a very unlikely place," she'd told the machine, her tone upbeat, as if she were about to share a compelling story. But the message ended, and she didn't leave any other details.

What the hell was she talking about? The library was closed now, so he'd have to wait until tomorrow to ask. He eyed the traffic as Ned merged onto the freeway. One distressing possibility is that she'd found a photo of Sam, a darker version of Mason who was way more in touch with his id. He'd conjured Sam on the Grapalia case, and the guy had done some worrisome things that Mason had got wind of, and possibly more that he didn't know about. Sam had disappeared again back then, but maybe, somehow, he'd returned.

Five

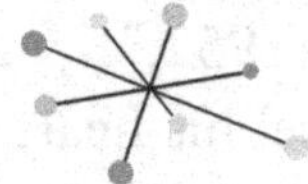

IN THE MORNING MASON woke when his body told him to, happy not to be roused by an alarm. It was still earlyish, and he stuck his head into Ned's office.

"Want some breakfast?"

"I did that hours ago," Ned said, raising his eyebrows.

"Suit yourself."

In the kitchen Mason made a pot of espresso, then ate some fruit, then another pot of espresso to take out on the balcony with him. It was chilly out here, but it was nice to sit in the muted daylight, the mist starting to burn off from the surrounding hilly neighborhoods. Once he felt fully lucid, he pulled out his phone and dialed the history department at the library.

He recognized Harmony's voice when she picked up.

"So what kind of photo of me did you find?"

"I was doing facial recognition runs on old pictures in the library's collection," she said, "and there you were."

"How old are these pictures?"

"I found you in 1952."

Mason could feel his heart pounding. "Obviously it's not me. I wasn't born yet."

"I know that, man—come on. I just thought it was interesting that you have a doppelgänger from back then."

"Why were you comparing photos of me?"

"We just got this new software," Harmony said. "I was messing around with it, and ran some pictures from my phone. You and me and Gilbert. Yours was the only face that popped up in the historical images."

"That's so bizarre."

"I can send you the picture, if you want."

"Can I come down and see you?"

"Of course. That's what the 'public' in public library means. You know where to find me."

Mason went inside and pulled on his jacket, and made sure his laptop was in his backpack before he slung it on. After he kissed Ned good-bye, he cycled down the hill and took the train downtown. Once he'd locked up his wheels outside the central library, he strode into the grand building and walked down the escalators to the history department, on the lowest floor.

Harmony was parked behind the reference desk when he walked up. He hadn't seen her in a while—she'd dyed some henna red into her dreads, piled elegantly on her head. When she looked up and recognized him, she rose and leaned across the counter to exchange an air kiss.

"You look great," Mason said.

"Back at you. You look the same as you did in 1952."

"It's not me," he said intently. "You have to show me this photo."

Harmony chuckled as she lifted her monitor onto the counter, then pulled up the image. They both leaned in to peer at the screen. It was black-and-white, depicting a small group of people standing on a curb next to a streetlamp, likely waiting for the light to change so they could cross the street. Even though it was impossible to see his distinctive coloring, he recognized himself instantly, wearing his fedora and the suit that at this moment was hanging in his closet. In the photo he could even make out the hibiscus print of his necktie. Standing at the back of the group, he was taller than anyone else, and that made his features clearly visible.

The expression on his face was distant, like he was concentrating, trying to figure something out, or maybe he was worried. That made sense—it took a lot of work to navigate that place.

"The metadata says it was taken outside the Baltimore Hotel in 1952 or 1953. There aren't any names or anything. It's just a slice-of-life photo."

"Who took it?"

"There's no name for the photographer, just the collection. It came from a newspaper archive."

"The *Bugle*?"

"One of the defunct newspapers. Everything in its archive and its morgue got donated to the public library when it folded in the 1980s."

"I wonder who he is," Mason said, eyeing the photo again.

"Maybe that's your grandfather."

"Neither of them looked like me." He met Harmony's gaze. "So why is the library doing facial recognition?"

"I probably shouldn't be using my own pictures," she said. "The idea is to stitch things together through the decades. To see if people overlap. So far we've found some faces from a labor protest in the postwar era who turned up at other events in the 1960s. That way we might be able to put names to some of the faces in old photos, and illuminate the circumstances of what people were doing."

"I can see the utility in that." Mason straightened up. "Thanks for showing me."

"I'll send you a copy," she said, and waved as Mason left.

Walking up the escalators to the ground level, he thought about that day. It could have been any one of several days, not that long ago for Mason, when he'd bled through to that era. There wasn't really a risk of his bleed-throughs being exposed, he decided. He still had that necktie, but no one would think he'd actually been there. Most people would make the assumption that Harmony had made: it was just a coincidence that he had the same features as someone who lived so long ago.

Unlocking his bicycle, he thought about that time, and the way people looked. The cumbersome clothes, the sooty air, the segregation. Back then he and Harmony would have been in very different neighborhoods, and likely never would have met.

Mason cycled the few blocks to his office. Once he was upstairs, he eyed the VCR. Time to see what was on that tape. He moved the machine to his desk and connected it to his computer monitor. It took a few minutes to sort out the wires and get it running. The tape had already been rewound—the machine must have done that itself, when he'd been sleeping, when it recorded right to the end.

When he pressed PLAY, his screen was overwhelmed with a low-resolution image of blue-and-white static—an electronic snowstorm. Mason picked up *Beyond the Dial* again. The author advised skipping the first half hour of the tape, as you wouldn't have been in deep enough sleep, and then to fast-forward through the entire recording, watching for unusual patterns on the screen.

That would certainly speed things up, he thought, and hit the fast-forward button, peering intently at the monitor. After a few minutes he had to stop to rest his eyes. The static was harder to look at than he'd imagined.

At one point he thought he saw an unusual flicker, so he stopped the tape and rewound it a little, and watched the recording at normal speed. There was nothing exceptional to see, just the electronic snow. As he watched he could see patterns forming in it, rectangles and circles and ovals, but he knew that was just the mechanical part of his brain trying to make sense of the random input.

Fast-forwarding again, his focus inevitably wandered, and he was only partly paying attention to the monitor when he saw a face, just for an instant, rising from the noise. A woman, with gray hair and the lines of age. She was grinning, and looking right at him.

Snapping upright, he rewound the tape and watched that part, first at regular speed and then in fast-forward, but she didn't appear again, even when he rolled the tape in slow mode. Before long he hit the end of the recording, and sat back to rub his eyes. All that static was giving him a migraine.

There was another way—his regular psychic technique. He moved over to the lounge chair next to the sofa and got comfortable, then closed his eyes and cleared his mind. It wasn't always an effective way to gain insight or make decisions, and often the information was ambiguous to the rational part of his mind, but he usually got something.

As he sat there, focused on the void, he had the sensation of being bodily pulled toward something, and at the same time dropping down a few feet. It was like someone had grabbed his arm and pulled him off a stepstool. Usually the technique just picked up information drifting in, images and sounds and general impressions, so the experience felt odd, but he resisted the urge to pull away from it, and let it happen.

The next sensation he got was audible, with no associated imagery—a sustained deep hiss. The audio equivalent of the electronic snow, perhaps? But it was something more than that. It made him think of how the wind sounded blowing through a pine forest, like camping up at Big Bear or on the Kaibab Plateau. Then came a woman's voice, almost a sigh, but her words were discernable in the wind: *I've been waiting and waiting.*

Mason took a breath and quickly opened his eyes. That part had been so vivid that it left his heart pounding. The breathy voice didn't belong to anyone he recognized. Maybe it was something else—symbolic of an idea, maybe, rather than a person. But as it often went, the information felt vague, like his rational mind couldn't really draw any conclusions.

Rising, he wheeled his bicycle through the office door, and locked it behind him, then rode the elevator to the lobby. He carried his steed down into the metro and stood with it on the train, headed home.

Watching the concrete walls of the tunnel flash past, he thought about that old-timey street photo of him. It wasn't all that difficult, being there, or rather, then. Like traveling abroad, maybe. It was a little uncomfortable, especially at first, and you had to learn new things, like how to ride the streetcar, and where to get lunch, and not to forget your hat. But unlike tramping around Europe, he already spoke the language.

He was going to do it, he decided. He was

going to go back and try to nudge Geraldine—to save her.

His phone rang, and he shifted with the sway of the train to put his other hand on his handlebars while he dug it out of his pants to look. The call was from Hanh's shop. It was rare to hear from her—she only called when she needed help from him and Matt with psychic stuff. No way was it a coincidence that she was calling him in the same moment he'd decided to ask for her help to get to the 1950s.

"You need a manicure," Hanh said when he picked up.

Mason frowned, unable to glance at his nails with his hands full. "I don't actually think I do."

"Even so, you should stop by today."

"What a coincidence," he said flatly. "I'm already on the metro."

"So I'll see you soon."

Tucking his phone away, he rode past his own stop and into Hollywood, then climbed up the long stairway to the street. From here it was just a few blocks to Hanh's nail salon. It was in a small strip mall on Sunset, and he locked his bicycle to a street sign along the boulevard, then strode through the parking lot to the doorway under the big red letters that said PRETTY NAIL BLOWOUT.

The woman on the reception desk beamed at him as he walked in.

"Mr. Mason—you can go back."

The place felt busy today, with manicurists and customers at most of the stations. As he walked through, several of the workers looked up at him. One said something in Vietnamese, and several others tittered in response. Mason could feel his face heating up. Something about his complexion always amused them. How could he be the only redhead who ever came in here?

Hanh stepped out of the back room and waved him over to an open nail station. She was petite and wore her black hair is a severe wedge. When they'd first met he thought she never smiled, but as they got to know each other, she'd started to loosen up.

Mason dropped into the chair across the little table from her, setting his backpack between his feet. She gestured for his hands, taking hold of them and looking them over.

"These aren't too bad," she said.

"They don't really need work, do they?"

"Let me give you a trim."

As Hanh set to work with her little clipper, he waited for her to speak. Watching her deftly snip his nails, he thought it was reminiscent of the plot to a samurai tale, or a kung-fu movie, where the most powerful warrior in the village was in disguise as a medieval rice farmer or a poor merchant. Hanh was so much more than a manicurist—he knew what she was capable of, effortlessly moving through time the way he moved around his house. He and Matt had decided she had some supervisory role in paranormal phenomena. This business-owner persona was definitely not her most authentic self.

Finally Hanh met his gaze. "So you're planning an excursion."

"I've only thought about it. I haven't done anything yet to put it into action."

She scoffed. "Thoughts are actions."

"So you're aware of the details?"

Hanh gestured for his other hand. "When you bleed through, the things you do can have unintended consequences. The world won't be the same when you get back."

"I realize that's a risk. How much could things change?"

"A lot." She looked up at him again. "But I know you're determined. The course of your excursion is already in motion." Hanh gestured vaguely in the air. "Over here and over there."

"You once said I relish this stuff," Mason said.

"You know you do."

"Doesn't that imply that I should pursue it?" Mason said. "Maybe I'll achieve something worthwhile."

"You know you're in a unique position. Threads untwine and twist together all the time, but do you realize how unusual it is to be able to split threads so far from your own? What if anyone could just bleed through and change whatever they wanted?"

"I guess things would get awfully confusing."

"How much revision to your current reality are you willing to risk?"

"What exactly might change?"

"You won't know that until you do it."

"You must already know." Mason sighed. "I'm thinking reality can't be so fragile that I could damage it on my own, right? I just want to give that woman a chance to finish what she started. To interview some saucer-heads and write about the space brothers. I doubt that extending her existence will break anything."

"Is there anything I could say that would discourage you?"

"Of course." He shrugged. "Just say no. I can't do it without you."

"You underestimate your power. It's like a boulder rolling down a hill. Everyone just needs to get out of your way. Why are Westerners so stubborn?"

Mason thought about that as she switched to an emery board to buff his nails.

"I'm not sure it's culturally specific," he said finally. "Ho Chi Minh was stubborn, and he changed history."

"Do not compare yourself to Ho Chi Minh," she said firmly. "And do not plan on rewriting history."

"I wouldn't do that."

"It's exactly what you plan to do. Things are already changing. Can't you feel it?"

"I kind of just decided to do this. Right before you called."

Hanh set her tools aside, and Mason reclaimed his hand, lifting it off the worktable.

"Some unusual things were happening when you were in Landers, correct?"

He nodded. "Unusual lights in the sky, and pale orbs in the landscape. Plus a weirdly large coyote."

"So disturbance is already happening because of this excursion you're planning. It's stretching the fabric of reality. Things are bleeding through the thin spots."

His eyebrows shot up. "That means it's already underway."

"Why are you surprised that you have that power? Our thoughts are what the world is made of."

"So I caused all that stuff."

"Not on your own. It's about you, and me, and Geraldine, although you're the one who's swinging the claymore."

Mason frowned. "What's a claymore?"

"Aren't your people from Scotland? That's where the redheads are."

"Not all of them. My family was English, although English people say my surname is really Danish."

"I just meant that you're the one who's hell-bent on this plan." She folded her arms. "Maybe you can do something for me to mitigate your momentum. Even things out a little. Then we'll talk about Geraldine."

"So you'll help me go, if I help you first?"

Hanh raised an eyebrow. "That is the implication."

"That's very good news." Mason had to smile. "What do you need me to do?"

"Go to a wedding, and throw a grenade."

He hesitated. "An actual grenade?"

"That wouldn't work. An emotional one." She frowned. "You think I'd get you to literally blow up a wedding?"

"Probably not."

She scoffed. "You'll fit in with this crowd. I'll get you invited as a cousin of one of the principals."

"I'm assuming I won't know anyone, and no one will recognize me. Are you sure it'll work? And what will I have to do?"

"If anyone asks, you're related to Martin's mother."

"Oh, god," Mason muttered. This was starting to feel like work. He reached for his backpack, and pulled out a notepad and a pen. As he jotted down the details, he said, "How will that explain my presence?"

"It's a complex family. There was an estrangement."

"Between Martin and his mother?"

"You won't need the details. It's a waste of brain cells."

"So I'm a cousin of Martin's on his mother's side." He looked up and met her gaze. "What kind of emotional grenade?"

"You just need to stir things up a little. Get some of the guests competing with one other. Emotions will flare. That should have the desired effect."

"So many questions," Mason said, but before he could ask, the woman from the front desk appeared, and said something in Vietnamese.

"I have another client," Hanh said.

"Of course." Mason rose and tucked his notepad into his bag, then pulled it on his shoulder. "So I'll hear from you?"

"You'll hear from the happy couple first."

Walking out into the daylight, lost in his thoughts, he unchained his bicycle. A bus pulled up beside him and opened its doors. This route plied the length of Sunset, and would take him most of the way home. He hustled to the front and pushed his bicycle into the street, then pulled down the bike rack to load his wheels.

It seemed like an odd request, he thought, once he'd boarded and found a seat, gazing out the window. Messing up a wedding sounded like it might be embarrassing too. But Hanh must have a good reason, and best of all, she was going to help him with the Geraldine situation. Wedding guests competing with one other, she'd said. That sounded familiar. He'd definitely read something like that.

Once he was in his own neighborhood, and he'd retrieved his bicycle from the front of the bus, he cycled up the hill, sweating and breathing hard by the time he walked into the house. Ned was in the kitchen, his apron on, working on dinner.

"Do you need my help?" Mason said, leaning on the counter.

Ned grinned. "You're fine. We'll eat soon. Eggplant in a spicy sauce. It's just you and me—Peggy's at Matt's tonight."

Relieved to be excused from the work, Mason went into the office and stood in front of the bookcase until he found the familiar volume about Greek mythology, then went back to the living room and stretched out on the sofa. The index had a couple of entries under "wedding," and he scanned the related stories.

Finally he found the one that had tweaked his memory: the goddess Eris had crashed a wedding, and threw a golden apple among the guests as a prize for the most beautiful. Three of the goddesses all thought it belonged to them, and Paris was appointed to arbitrate and choose the winner. He picked Aphrodite, and that started the Trojan War.

"I forgot to tell you," Ned called from the kitchen. "There was a letter for you."

"Not just bills and junk mail?"

"It's much more exotic than that."

Mason got up and went to the counter, where he climbed onto one of the barstools and reached for the pile of mail. The item Ned was talking about was on top—a lavender envelope, with Mason's name and address handwritten in elegant blocky letters.

"Did you smell it?" Ned said, eyeing him as he stirred the contents of the wok.

"Seriously?" Mason held it to his nose and sniffed. "Someone doused it with perfume."

"I think it's patchouli."

He tore open the envelope to find a wedding invitation. Hanh had somehow put this in motion retroactively, since they'd talked just a short time ago. But then she wasn't constrained by the flow of time.

"So what is it?" Ned said.

"An invite to a wedding."

"Who's getting hitched? Is it this summer?"

"It's this Saturday."

"That's pretty short notice," Ned said. "Whose wedding?"

"Uh …" Mason hesitated, pretending to study the invitation, trying to think fast. "It's a cousin of mine from back east."

"That Sam guy? We haven't seen him for a while."

"A different part of the family. I don't know them very well."

"It's nice to be invited, at least."

"Oh, I'm going."

Ned glanced at him, his brow furrowing. "Is it in town?"

"It's in Massachusetts."

"Why would they give you three days' notice when it's on the other side of the country?"

"You know what's happened to the post office lately," Mason said. "Maybe it's my fault. I might have overlooked the save-the-date email."

"Who is this cousin?"

"Martin. We're related through his mother."

Ned wiped his hands on his apron and stepped over to the counter. He reached for the invitation and scanned it.

"It's in the Berkshires," he said. "It's beautiful

there in the warm months."

"Come with me, if you want. It says plus one."

"I can't. I've got meetings Thursday and Friday." Ned went back to the stove and picked up the tongs, flipping pieces of eggplant in the wok. "If you're really going, you'll have to travel one of those days."

"I guess I'll have to figure that out."

"Why do you want to go? I've never heard you talk about this cousin."

"I guess because it's family."

Ned eyed him. "I'm only going to say this once. Anglos are so freaking weird."

"I've heard you say that many, many times, sweets."

"When's the last time you saw this guy? And who's he marrying?"

"It's been a while. I don't know who the bride is. I assume she'll be the one in the white dress."

"Wrong," Ned said flatly. "It's a boy-boy wedding. Didn't you notice that?" He picked up the invite again and read the names. "Martin Swithenbank and Henry Rao. I'd bet cash money that Henry is a dude. That surname is either Indian or Chinese, but Swithenbank sounds like your name: pasty and oat-fed and Anglo."

Mason took it from him and read it again. "Sure enough. Martin and I have more in common than I thought. I'll fit right in."

"You realize that going to a wedding across the country on such short notice is pretty weird. Even for you."

"I can see how the situation might appear that way, from your perspective."

Ned chuckled and went back to the wok.

"After dinner, will you help me book a flight?" Mason said. "You're canny with that stuff."

"You should RSVP first, and make sure they still want you. It's awfully late to be planning the meals and the seating. And see if you can get a room at that hotel on Friday, and probably Saturday night too. You don't want to be rushing to the airport the same afternoon as the event."

"Good idea."

Mason grabbed his laptop and sat at the dining table, and went to the site to RSVP. It seemed to accept it, and gave him a link to the hotel where the wedding was being held. There were still rooms available for the attendees, so he booked one for both nights.

The spicy eggplant was delicious, and after they'd cleaned up, Mason followed Ned to his desk, where he sat and waggled his mouse to wake his computer.

"There's no airport in that town," Ned said, after he'd poked around, peering at the screen. "You'll need a car no matter what. You can't even get close to there on a nonstop."

"What are the closest airports?"

"Hartford or Albany. Both are about an hour's drive."

"Which one has the cheapest cars?"

They finally decided on Albany, and Ned checked on flight times. The best option was taking the red-eye to the East.

"Give me your credit card," he said, and once Mason had retrieved it, he typed in the number, then eyed him. "Last chance to back out. Are you absolutely sure you want to do this? Getting there is going to be an overnight ordeal."

"Buy it," he said. "I already RSVP'd."

Later, in bed, as he was drifting into the hypnagogic state, Mason saw a golden ball. An apple, he realized—the apple of discord, from the story of Eris. He worked to bring himself to lucidity, so that he could take hold of it, and see what was written on it. But he couldn't quite get there, couldn't take charge of it, and he lost the image.

Six

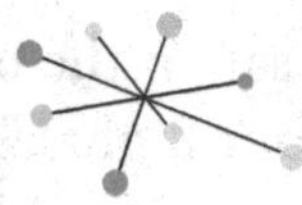

THE HOUSE WAS QUIET when Mason woke. Ned and Peggy were both gone. He made java and then had some fruit, and once he was sufficiently lucid, slung on his backpack and rode down the hill to cycle toward Hollywood, to Hanh's shop. He didn't need to check with her first—he knew she'd be around.

"Miss Hanh is finishing up with a client," the woman on the front desk told him. "Can you wait a moment?"

Mason had barely sat down on the puffy vinyl sofa when Hanh appeared, and waved him back. He followed her into the stock room, where there was a big sink, and open shelves lined with towels and bottles of chemicals, and a lunch table.

"Coffee?" Hanh said, and when he nodded, she took two mugs and poured dark liquid from the carafe of the battered coffeemaker that sat next to the sink.

When she handed him one, he saw that it had a chip in the rim, so he turned it around to drink from the opposite side. It didn't taste all that bad, although it probably got gnarlier as the day wore on and it sat on the burner.

"You booked your flights," Hanh said, dropping into a chair across the table and cradling her mug.

Mason wasn't sure if that was a question or not. "I did, and I RSVP'd."

"The snow is already gone in New England. It'll be nice."

"You know this thing you're planning has the echo of a myth," Mason said. "Eris and the golden apple."

"That woman was a handful," Hanh said, and sipped her coffee. "Quite the troublemaker."

"My role is the same, isn't it? To sow discord at somebody's wedding. It's got me feeling a little uneasy."

"The outcome will be positive this time. Eris's actions led to the Trojan War. What you're going to do will prevent a similar calamity decades hence. So you're doing something constructive. Something worthwhile, to use your phrase."

"I guess I trust your judgment," Mason said. "So what exactly am I supposed to do, and how can I do it without completely embarrassing myself?"

She smiled. "Have you got your pen?"

Pulling out his notepad, he scrawled down the details as she outlined the plan.

WHEN HE LEFT HANH'S place, he cycled to the metro and rode it downtown, where he wheeled his bicycle into his building and up to his office. At his desk he spent some time researching the couple who were getting married, digging for details about them online.

Despite his distinctive surname, there wasn't much trace of Martin, but Henry was a lawyer, and there was a short bio and a portrait of him on the website of his law firm. He was in his thirties, maybe, and had black hair, and dark-rimmed eyeglasses, and a confident smirk. His firm was based in New York. It was hard to tell from the site if it was a white-shoe outfit, or a bunch of ambulance chasers, or somewhere in between.

It would be easy enough to figure out, he knew, if he did a bit of research, but maybe it didn't matter. Mason sat back and looked out the windows, gazing at the dramatic skyline of the Financial District. None of this mattered, he decided. He didn't need to know who these guys were. It would make the job easier if they were strangers.

It was time for his shrink appointment anyway, and he walked out to the elevators, and into the stairwell, and trotted up a flight. Directly above his office, Miss Cassie's space was identical in terms of the layout, but she had much better furniture and a slightly higher view. He'd found his own office after coming to hers for a while and admiring the building. It still wasn't clear to him how she felt about having a longtime client suddenly at such close proximity.

The sign on her door said COME IN, so he slid it across to read PLEASE KNOCK, then stepped inside. Miss Cassie rose from her desk to greet him. She was pushing sixty, and always looked sharp, despite the weight on her frame. Today she was dressed in a dark tailored suit, and she was letting her hair grow into a natural Afro, he saw, rather than straightening it. That must be the current style. It was so dark, though, that she likely still dyed it.

Mason dropped into one of the plush lounge chairs by the windows, and Miss Cassie sat on the sofa, facing him, her tablet in hand.

"It's good to see you," she said, and they talked through some of his ongoing stuff. Eventually she looked up from her notes. "So what else is happening? How's your work?"

"Slow, I'd have to say. But I'm going to a wedding in Massachusetts this weekend."

"And that's work-related?"

"It is—I don't know anyone who'll be there, but I'm supposed to break up the happy couple."

Her eyebrows shot up. "Someone hired you to do that?"

"In a way."

"And you're going to do it."

"I've been assured it's for the best."

Miss Cassie took a breath. "Is anything you're planning to do illegal?"

Mason frowned. "What, so you can report me to the cops? No way. I'm just going to mix things up a little, and see what happens."

"Weddings are supposed to be celebratory events. When we take pleasure in spoiling someone's happiness, that comes from aggression, and a sense of competitiveness."

"I don't think it'll be pleasurable," Mason said, "and I'm not competing with these people. It's just a job."

She set her tablet beside her on the sofa cushion. "Let's talk about your moral compass. What if a client hired you to cause someone else physical harm? Say they wanted you to push someone down a flight of stairs."

"I would never do that."

"How is trying to break up a couple at their wedding any different?"

Mason shrugged. "With what I'm doing, nobody gets hurt."

"Not physically, maybe, but there will be emotional damage."

"Maybe it's more like getting vaccinated. The needle hurts for a second, and you feel weird for a couple days, but then you don't get polio or measles."

Her brow furrowed, and her lips pressed into a hard line.

"Do you know the story of Eris and the judgment of Paris?" Mason said. "This job reminded me of that."

"You know what the outcome of that incident was."

"This won't be so dramatic. I just think it's interesting that mythology informs my work. The pattern echoes through it."

"Or maybe you're just using that story to allow yourself to be blithe about causing people harm." Miss Cassie sighed. "You need to think about the consequences of your actions." She glanced at the wall clock, then sat up. "So how much are you getting paid to do this?"

"It's a tit-for-tat type deal," Mason said, tucking his notepad into his bag. "I trash the wedding, then my client will help me do something I need to do."

"Well, take care of yourself," she said, rising. "And try to be kind."

"Can I take the back stairs?" Mason said, slinging his bag on his shoulder.

Miss Cassie frowned but waved her assent, and he went to the stairwell in the corner, and flipped the deadbolt, and stepped in, trotting down the four quarter-flights as he admired the light fixture suspended in the middle. Digging out his keys, he unlocked the back door into his own office.

It seemed odd that Miss Cassie was intent on him being kind. That had never come up before, and really, it had nothing to do with the job he was doing. Grabbing his bicycle, he wheeled it out the front door, and took the elevator down, then cycled to a stationery store in the neighborhood.

Hanh's plan involved lavender paper, like the wedding invitation, and in the shop he found a set of notes and envelopes that looked similar in size and color. Once he'd paid for it, he cycled to the metro and went home.

Peggy was in the kitchen, wearing her apron, stained with the effort of many meals. He could hear Ned's voice in the office, on a business call, it sounded like, even though it was late in the day.

"It smells amazing in here," Mason said, stepping over to the counter.

"I'm making gyoza for dinner."

"Do you need a hand?"

Peggy grinned. "I don't. But have a seat, if you want."

She was wise not to get him involved, he thought, climbing onto a barstool. He didn't have the finesse for kitchen work. Ned had once said it was like watching an orangutan trying to put a wristwatch together. That wasn't even insulting, because Mason knew it was true.

"The music was great the other night," he said.

"It was a little odd to play a venue with no one in it," Peggy said. She moved her mixing bowl over to the counter, closer to him, and they chatted about her performance. "Ned says you're going to a wedding in Connecticut?"

"Close—it's in western Massachusetts. I actually need your design skills. I have to make a card for the event."

"I can probably help with that." Peggy spooned a bit of filling into a flat wrapper and folded it closed, then quickly crimped the edges together. "Why are you going on such short notice?"

"Psychic work," he said quietly, glancing over his shoulder to make sure Ned was out of earshot. "Hanh asked me to go."

"Ned doesn't know that part, I'm thinking."

"I don't think he could handle it."

"I hate being in the middle of your lies," she

said, glancing up at him as she filled another wrapper.

"It's not a lie. Just compartmentalized information."

"You shouldn't be treating your boyfriend like you're the CIA."

"Do you think he could handle the full version?" Mason demanded. "That my nail salon-owning psychic mentor asked me to go to a wedding where I don't know anyone, on the other side of the country?"

Peggy sighed. "Probably not. Do you even know why you're going?"

"To stir things up in a way that will prevent some future negative event. I don't know what, exactly, but in Hanh's words, it's 'decades hence.'"

Ned wandered out, and stood beside Mason, and leaned in to kiss him.

"Need a sous-chef?" he said, eyeing Peggy.

"Can you shred the daikon?"

He stepped into the kitchen and pulled on his apron. "So are you ready for the wedding?"

"Peggy's going to help me make a card tonight," Mason said. "Other than that I'll just need my suit and a change of underpants."

"You might want to pack a toothbrush," Ned said, waving the grater. "And are you not taking a gift?"

"I hadn't planned to."

"You have to take a gift. It compensates for your dinner. Stuff some cash in your card, at least."

"That's probably a good idea," Mason said, and stood up.

In the bedroom he stretched out on the bed, not really planning to drift off, but it happened anyway. Peggy woke him a while later, summoning him to the table.

"They're perfect," Mason said, admiring the crispy golden gyoza between his chopsticks. "I'm blown away by all the flavors. It's like a symphony."

"There's not too much cabbage?" Peggy said.

"It gives them the crunch."

She nodded, satisfied. "That's the intention."

"Where's the daikon?"

"In the dipping sauce," she said. "That's what gives it body."

After dinner, once the kitchen was in order, Ned eyed them both. "If you two are going to work, I'm going to listen to music."

"It's an album night?" Mason said.

"Duke Ellington."

Ned liked to play through a whole album and just listen to it, with no screens, no chitchat, no distractions. It was more focus than Mason could muster, so Ned was usually left to it on his own. Mason grabbed his backpack and followed Peggy into her bedroom. She got settled at her desk, and he sat nearby, on the end of her bed.

"So what are we doing?" she said.

Mason handed her the wedding invitation. "Can you emulate that handwriting?"

"Probably." She looked it over, then held it to her nose and sniffed. "*Oh, là là.* Is that patchouli?"

"Do you have any perfume like that?"

"I have some sandalwood oil. It's similar."

"Great." Mason pulled out the packet of lavender stationery. "On the notepaper, I want to write, 'You're the only man I ever truly loved. Thanks for being here.'"

Peggy eyed him for a moment, and bit her lip. The muffled strains of jazz were audible from the living room.

"Should I ask?" she said finally.

Mason shook his head. "It's so hard to explain."

In her desk drawer she dug through her pens and pencils, and chose one that she uncapped and then tested on a sheet of printer paper. Eyeing the scented envelope, she practiced the blocky letters: *You're the only man …*

"Such an interesting message," she said, "considering you don't know anyone at this wedding."

"It's a whole thing. Explaining it would be difficult."

"OK," Peggy said flatly, her brow furrowing.

"It's not that I'm trying to be deceptive. I'd call it the classic psychic's dilemma: how do I bring metaphysical experiences back into basic consensus reality?"

"I guess I should be grateful that you're not willing to blow my basic mind."

After a few more practice lines, she wrote the words on one of the lavender sheets, then handed it to him.

"How's that?"

"Brilliant. Then we need to do the envelope."

Peggy slid one of the lavender envelopes out of the packet. "What do I write on it?"

"It has to be in big letters: 'To the hottie.'"

She scoffed and chose another pen with a thicker tip, deftly inscribing the words.

"Right on," Mason said, admiring her work, and waited while she went to find the sandal-wood oil.

When she sat down again, she wiped the little vial around the edges of the note, then folded it into the envelope, and handed it to Mason. He held it to his nose.

"I can't tell the difference from the patchouli. You're a genius."

"It's pretty ripe," she said. "I hope they let you through airport security with that."

☩

ON THURSDAY MORNING MASON decided that Ned was probably right: there was more to prepare than just a change of underpants. He spent some time putting together his toiletries and clothes, and then tucked his vintage 1950s suit into a garment bag. The rest of his stuff fit easily in the bottom, which meant he'd only need to carry that plus his backpack.

In the late afternoon he took a disco nap to bank some sleep hours in advance—taking the red-eye meant it would be a short night for him. Peggy was out for the evening, and Ned prepared Salisbury steak made from seitan, with a perfectly thin brown sauce. After they'd eaten, Ned sat back in his chair.

"Are you all packed?"

"I'm ready to go when you are."

"So the only question is whether you want to show up at LAX in sporty style or in town-car style."

"If we took the Crown Vic," Mason said, "I'd want to sit in the back. For the true town-car experience."

Ned nodded. "That means it's the Barracuda. I'm not your damn chauffeur."

Mason gathered his things and walked outside, holding the garment bag over his shoulder while he waited for Ned to back the Barracuda out of the garage. Once he'd set his stuff in the trunk and climbed in, Ned navigated toward the freeway, the car's big throaty engine rumbling as it accelerated up the ramp.

"You know how crazy this trip is, right?" Ned said.

"I have to admit that it does feel just a little crazy."

"You can still back out."

"I've got momentum now," Mason said. "I'm going to make the best of it."

"At least you'll meet some relatives you haven't seen in a while." Ned glanced at his mirror as he changed lanes. "It might even be fun."

Soon they were winding around the snarl of roadways at LAX, and Ned pulled up to the curb at his terminal. Mason leaned in to kiss him good-bye, and Ned ran a hand into his hair.

"I'll miss you," he said softly. "Call me tomorrow."

"I'll be back in a flash," he said, and climbed out.

Taking a night flight felt more mellow than the daytime version. The passengers were more subdued so late in the evening, not all caffeinated and antsy and yanged out. Once the plane was in the air, the crew blacked out the cabin, on the assumption that people would want to sleep. Shifting in his seat to get as comfortable as he could, it didn't take him long to get there.

Seven

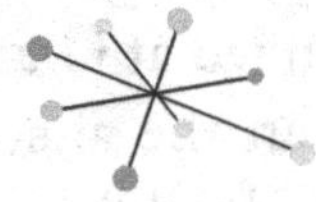

WHEN MASON WOKE AGAIN it was to a muffled announcement and daylight streaming in the little windows. The crew's words were garbled but he took it that they'd be landing soon. He smiled at his seatmate as he sat up, but she avoided his gaze and glanced sidelong at his shirt. There was a wet spot on it, he realized—he'd been drooling in his sleep.

Once he'd wiped his mouth, he stretched and did a neck roll. It was a little embarrassing, but he wasn't worried that she was grossed out. Someone had once told him, "You can be as eccentric as you want until you start scaring people." He wasn't at that point quite yet.

The Philly airport looked like all the airports, he saw, walking through it to his connecting flight. The light outside the windows was a little different—bluer, maybe, and hazy, the way it always was east of the Rockies.

Once he'd boarded the next plane he decided to pay for Wi-Fi rather than sleep, despite his abbreviated night. He pulled out his laptop and read more about the flying-saucer meetings that Geraldine had attended at Giant Rock.

The guy who ran the airstrip out there and hosted the events had published some books, but more interesting than that was his FBI file. Several hundred pages of it had been released, the result of some saucer-head's FOIA request, and it was all online. Once he'd downloaded it, Mason dug in.

The feds had been skeptical from the beginning. The file outlined how the guy hosted the meet-ups and channeled messages from aliens, but because his ideas were so out-there for the time, several suspicious citizens had made reports to the FBI, accusing him of being a communist. It was a time of fear and political witch hunts, when people's careers were ruined by the mere accusation of involvement with the commies, but the feds never hounded this guy the way they had gone after people in other fields. It made sense—nothing about the Giant Rock meet-ups was about that kind of politics.

Mason downloaded one of the guy's books and skimmed through it. In it he linked the space brothers with Christianity, almost to the point that it felt like he was trying to jumpstart his own religion. It had never caught on, it seemed, and there was no trace of a modern iteration of the group.

Nothing in the Giant Rock material mentioned Landers by name, so he pulled up a page about the history of the place. It hadn't even been called that until 1962—that was definitely something he should remember, if he was going to wind up there a decade earlier.

One of the newspaper articles about Geraldine had described her car, he remembered, and scanning it now, it mentioned the make and model, and that it was dark red. He found photos of the same kind of vehicle online, and studied them closely, noting its curves and lines, the look of the trunk, the shape of the grille. If he was going to follow Geraldine around, he needed to be able to recognize her ride.

The friend who took Geraldine's cat was named Margaret, described in the newspaper article as a singer. When he searched for her name, it appeared that she had been a somewhat prominent person in the city in those days. There was a photo of her rubbing shoulders with the governor, and another of her singing at some black-tie charity event.

One online source that mentioned Margaret was a rundown of a court case. Acting as the executor of a woman's estate, Margaret had sued the surviving husband. Mason couldn't understand the legalese, or what the suit was even about, specifically, but the judgment in the case somehow set a precedent in California law. The surname of the woman who'd died was Reade—how strange was it that Geraldine's surname, Reed, was so similar? Margaret must have felt that, the synchronicity, the odd coincidence that two of her prematurely deceased friends had almost the same name.

The chime sounded and the crew announced that they were getting ready to land. Mason tucked his computer away and gazed out the window as the ground gradually came closer. The landscape was lush with that pale yellowy green of spring's new growth. There was so much life here, such exuberance, even this early in the season.

Once he'd filed out of the cramped cabin with everybody else, he found the car-rental desk, and when it was his turn, he set his credit card and driver's license on the counter for the clerk. The guy had his dark hair in a stylish pomp and beamed at him as he stepped over.

"You came from California today?" he said, as he glanced at Mason's license and swiped it into his computer.

"I actually left last night. On the red-eye to Philly."

"Ouch," he said, and frowned sympathetically, then peered at his screen. "So—we're out of subcompacts. I'll upgrade you to a larger vehicle. Of course there's no charge."

"What kind of larger vehicle?"

"I've got a Land Rover."

"That sounds awfully big," Mason said.

"It's a great car." He looked up. "It's also your only option, unless you want a minivan."

"No vans. Can I look at it first?"

He nodded confidently. "We'll go outside."

The decision had been finalized already, Mason realized, as the guy printed out the paperwork, and tore it off the printer, and had him sign it.

Following him out the big doors into the daylight, Mason inhaled sharply at the shock of cold air. The intense frigid humidity felt like being slapped. How could the landscape be so green when the air was this cold?

"This is it," the guy said, pointing out a silverygray behemoth.

"I can't drive that. It's the size of a dump truck."

"You'll get used to it."

"It must get, what, like, four miles to the gallon?"

"Gas is cheaper here than in California." He waved a hand and sighed impatiently. "Most people are happy to get the upgrade."

"If there's no other choice, I guess I'll make it work. Maybe the size won't matter so much on the freeway."

"We don't have freeways here," he said, handing him the keys. "We call them turnpikes and interstates."

"Good to know," Mason said. "Is there an empty parking lot where I can practice?"

He laughed, his tone deep. "It's not a big rig. Just don't try to park in a stall marked 'compact.' You'll be fine."

The guy went back inside the terminal, and Mason spent some time adjusting the seat and the mirrors and looking over the controls before he finally pulled onto the street. It was only nerve-racking for the first few minutes, and being so high up actually felt safer. The roads were in good shape here, but the vehicle rode rough, considering how big it was.

The navigation on his phone directed him onto the freeway, and soon he was headed east. It rained a little, big drops spattering on the windshield, and it took him a moment to find the wipers. No one else on the freeway seemed to be bothered enough to slow down or put their headlights on.

The greenery really was amazing, so copious and extensive, even along the road. It made things look cleaner and less crowded than in LA. The first half of the ride last week on the way to the Mojave was much less calming—a whole lot of concrete and asphalt and dusty brown hillsides.

The rain stopped before he got to Pittsfield, where he got off the freeway. He could see densely forested hills in the distance. Those had to be the mountains Ned was talking about. But that's not where he was headed, and he focused on navigating the town.

The hotel looked newish, he thought, as he pulled into the parking lot. Upscale but not luxurious. When he climbed out of the car, the air was still damp and chilly, but it didn't feel like the assault he'd endured in Albany. It took him a second of peering at the key fob to figure out how to lock the vehicle, and once he had, he strode toward the lobby.

A signboard inside the doors said CONGRATULATIONS MARTIN AND HENRY below a photo of the pair of them. Mason paused to look. They were both smiling and professionally posed. Online he'd seen Henry, with his South Asian complexion, looking about the same as in this photo. Martin definitely looked Anglo, with mousy brown hair and freckles, sporting a little bow tie and glasses with strangely large lenses. If that was the style now, Mason had never noticed it.

At the front desk, he waited for the clerk to step over.

"Am I too early to check in?"

"You're fine," she said, and he handed over his license and a credit card.

"No baggage?" She glanced at him as she went to her computer.

"It's in my car. I wanted to make sure you'd have me first."

She peered at her screen, and then gestured to the little input pad.

"What percentage of the hotel is booked for the wedding?" Mason said, grabbing the stylus to sign his name.

"All of it." She raised her eyebrows. "So you'll know everyone here."

As he was tucking his cards away, waiting for her to produce the room key, a woman stepped up beside him. She was curvy and had her dark hair pulled back.

"There's no remote for the TV in my room," she said to the clerk.

"Let me grab you another." She set Mason's card key on the counter. "Top floor, left off the elevator," she said, meeting his gaze, and then stepped into the back.

"Did you drive up from the city for the happy event?" the woman said, looking him over.

Mason turned toward her. "I came from Los Angeles, but I only had to drive from Albany. You came from Boston?"

She smiled. "In this part of the world 'the city' means New York."

"Good to know. I'm Mason, by the way."

"Tanisha."

"Born on Monday," Mason said, tucking his key away.

She frowned. "Now, how did you know that?"

"Are you asking because I'm a white guy?"

"Even black folks don't know that one."

"I'm not sure how I know. But I know it's originally African."

"That's such a shoehorned designation, don't you think? Do you have any idea how many ethnic groups there are on that continent?"

"Hundreds and hundreds," Mason said. "I backpacked around West Africa for a while after college."

"You're so much less boring than all these lawyers and accountants," she said, waving her arm. "My husband just flopped on the bed and started snoring. Do you want to get a drink?"

Mason laughed. "Absolutely."

The clerk returned with the TV remote, and

Tanisha took it and tucked it into her handbag, then pointed the way to the bar.

"I'm glad you mentioned your husband," Mason said. "Otherwise I'd think you were macking on me."

She laughed. "It's a boy-boy wedding. I'm working on the assumption that most of the guys here are gay."

"That's actually pretty good logic."

The barroom was empty at this hour, except for a lone couple at a table in the back, and he and Tanisha sat at the bar.

"What are we drinking?" the bartender said, stepping over to them.

After Tanisha ordered a martini, Mason said, "A gin and tonic for me. Don't be shy with the sauce—I've been on the road all day."

As the guy went to make their drinks, Tanisha swiveled toward him and frowned. "I thought you said you came from Albany. That's only an hour down the pike."

"I guess it felt like all day."

"So are you a friend of the groom, or the other groom?"

"I'm a cousin," Mason said.

"Definitely on Martin's side. You don't look like Henry's relatives."

"What do they look like?"

"They're Indians," she said, raising her

eyebrows. "Half of them just got off the plane from Mumbai."

"You're on Henry's side?"

"I'm married to one of Henry's work friends."

"Another lawyer," Mason said, eyeing her sidelong.

"My husband is, but I'm not. I'm in the classroom."

"I knew there was a reason I liked you. Teachers are usually people-oriented."

That elicited a laugh, and as their drinks arrived, she clinked her glass on Mason's.

"Do you want to charge these to your room?" the bartender said.

"Let me." Tanisha fished her room key out of her bag.

"What about you, Mason?" she said. "What do you do for work?"

"I'm a psychic investigator."

"Wow." Her eyes grew wide. "I wish they all could be California boys. You and I are definitely going to sit together tonight."

Mason chuckled. "What happens tonight?"

"It's the reception for the out-of-towners. I assume it'll be right here in the bar."

"So how did Henry and Martin meet?" he said, squeezing his lime wedge into his glass.

"I have no idea, but I can tell you those two are from different worlds. You'll see tonight. All of Martin's crowd is hipster trash. You probably knew that part. Henry's friends are establishment lawyers."

"So they're not trendy?"

"If you look up the word *boring* in the dictionary, there's a picture of Henry and the rest of the firm."

"And you're married to one," Mason said, his brow furrowing.

As they drank, Tanisha told him more of what she'd seen of the wedding guests. Eventually she pulled out her phone.

"I should go check on the old ball and chain," she said. "See you at the reception."

Mason slammed the last of his highball and walked out with her, then went to the parking lot to grab his bags. Once he was up in his room, and had hung his suit in the closet, he realized he was exhausted. It was partly from the gin but mostly from the short night, plus driving a big rig across two states. Ditching his clothes, he climbed into the bed, not even bothering to pull the drapes.

Eight

DAYLIGHT WAS FADING WHEN Mason came to consciousness, waking not because he was rested but because his stomach was grumbling. Scrabbling for his phone on the nightstand, he checked for local vegan food options. The restaurant that looked best to him said it wouldn't be open until Memorial Day, so he settled on a pizza joint that had vegan cheese.

Pulling on his clothes, he went out to the parking lot and drove the absurdly oversize car to the place, relieved to find room for it in the parking lot, and went in, and sat in a booth. The food was OK, but it always felt odd to be in a strange place, with no connection to it, no frame of reference.

Back at the hotel, he went up to his room, and had a shower, then put on his suit. He'd noticed several people headed into the bar—the reception must have started. Once he got downstairs and stepped into the barroom, he instantly regretted wearing the suit. No one else was dressed up. Most of the crowd looked just slightly older than college age. There were a few women here but mostly it was guys, and their conversations were loud, fueled by alcohol and familiarity.

Maybe the official reception hadn't started yet. Right now it was just about drinking and socializing, and everyone seemed to know everyone else. He maneuvered up to the bar and ordered a gin and tonic. Maybe if he had a drink in his hand he'd feel less like a misfit.

When his highball appeared, he pulled out a sawbuck and set it on the bar top.

"It's an open bar," the bartender told him.

Mason pocketed the ten and left him a single, then sipped his drink and leaned back, surveying the room. The freely flowing booze might explain why the place was already so boisterous.

"Who's the guy in the suit?" someone said, somewhere off to his right.

Mason didn't bother to look, but took a deep breath, then a slug of his drink, feeling his face heating up.

Before long Tanisha walked in, wearing a short dress with silvery sequins, cut low to show off her cleavage. That was a relief—he wasn't the only one who'd dressed up a little.

Tanisha spotted him and waved. For some reason she already had a drink in hand. Maybe there was an auxiliary bar in the lobby, or she'd raided the minibar. Walking over to join her, he watched her claim a table along the wall, then sat next to her on a banquette that faced the room.

"This is Martin's crowd," Tanisha said, leaning closer to be heard over the booze-fueled gabbing and the laughter. "It looks like they all know each other, but I don't know any of these people."

"Tell me about it, sister. I'm a stranger in a strange land myself."

She eyed him sidelong. "So you're an Old Testament kind of guy."

"Is that from the Old Testament? I thought it was from a science-fiction novel."

"It's probably both."

"Still, I didn't know it was Jesus-y," Mason said. "That stuff seems to permeate everything."

"The Old Testament's not actually about Jesus."

"Once again, who knew?"

Tanisha laughed. "I take it you're not religious."

"I had some exposure, but I didn't really absorb the minutiae."

"The psychic thing has to be similar," she said. "In the nineteenth century there was a whole religion based on talking to the spirits. They had a community upstate somewhere."

"I'm not that kind of psychic. My thing is more like science—a quest for information, not a template for behavior and social structure."

Tanisha sat up and waved toward the entrance. A tall guy wearing a black T-shirt met her gaze and walked toward them.

"My husband," she explained.

The guy was buff, and pleasantly filled out his shirt, and had a little mustache and slick black hair. Tanisha introduced him as Ray. He greeted Mason with an affable smile, then sat on the other side of her.

"You don't look like a lawyer," Mason said, leaning forward to meet his gaze.

Ray laughed. "What do lawyers look like?"

"More uptight, maybe. Less athletic. Like Henry."

"You're on Martin's side?"

"I'm related to Martin through his mother."

Ray nodded. "You don't seem like his airhead peers. I can see the family resemblance, though. The red hair."

Ray must know some stories about Martin's family, Mason realized. It would be interesting to hear the details, to learn why his mother was estranged, but like Hanh had said, he didn't really need to know.

The place was getting more crowded, and louder, and several people sat at their table, but it was only out of necessity, and they made no attempt to connect.

"Do you think the grooms are going to stop by?" Mason said, shouting to be heard.

"I doubt it," Tanisha said. "They have too much prep work to do."

"Henry said he'd try later on," Ray offered, leaning toward them.

That would probably work, Mason thought, considering what he had to do. He needed to get the lavender envelope circulating tonight, or in the morning—definitely before tomorrow's ceremony. But not just yet.

He chatted with Ray and Tanisha, and gossiped about the other guests, and watched the animated goings-on. After they'd had a second round, and the crowd was thinning out, Tanisha rose, and squeezed his hand to say good-night, and she and Ray left.

The only other person still at their table was a blond guy wearing trendy eyeglasses and a silky gold shirt. It had offset buttons like a chef's jacket.

Probably couture, Mason decided. The guy had chatted a little with Ray earlier, but now that it was just him and Mason, he pulled out his phone and stared at the screen.

"Which side are you with?" Mason said, leaning toward him.

The guy glanced up, as if noticing for the first time that Mason wasn't a piece of furniture. "Martin," he said, and looked back to his phone.

"I came from California today. I don't really know anyone here."

He briefly met Mason's gaze. "I live in San Francisco."

"What part of the city?" Mason said.

Again he looked up, his brow furrowing, as if he had more important things to focus on. "I live in San Francisco," he said flatly.

"Got it," Mason said, and nodded.

No way could he compete with whatever was on that little screen. Mason rose and carried his half-empty highball glass to the other end of the room, where there were a couple of tables pushed together, with a dozen or so people seated around them. The stragglers and dregs of the reception were coalescing here, and it was almost all guys. He greeted them with a nod, and sat in an open chair. Several of them glanced at him, but not with any interest, and continued their conversations.

Now that he was seated, no one was paying

him any attention. The conditions were right—this was his opportunity. Reaching into his jacket, he palmed the lavender envelope and set it in his lap, out of sight. Twisting around to the table behind him, he grabbed a little wooden bowl of mixed nuts and moved it to the table he was sitting at. He rose halfway from his chair as he tucked the envelope underneath the bowl, then set them near the middle of the table. No one even glanced at what he was doing. He took a handful of nuts to munch on and sat back.

Now he just had to wait. Surveying the guests, he tuned in to some of their conversations. Mostly it seemed to be about college, reminiscences about classes they'd been in together, and campus life. It seemed introspective, but maybe it was logical—college was their shared experience, and none of these guys were more than a few years past graduating.

They gossiped about clothes and romances and hookups. One of the loudest, sitting over on the left, was a wiry guy with thick black hair. His affected intonation was grating, as every sentence sounded like a complaint, his tone rising and falling in exaggerated contrast.

"Cassius almost didn't get out of first year," he said, eyeing the guy who was sitting directly opposite Mason.

Cassius was wearing red-rimmed glasses with

no lenses in them, and wore his hair in knobby twists. He thumped the tabletop with the heel of his fist.

"It's not my fault. They changed the grading system. None of them even considered how that would impact me."

The blond with the gold shirt stepped around the table and sat a few chairs to the right of Cassius. He'd put his phone away.

"That happened to me too," the blond said. "But I managed to roll with it."

The guy with the thick hair and the annoying voice waved a hand. "Because you were on your knees sucking faculty dick."

The blond scowled at him. "If you're talking about Professor Stockbridge, we were very much in love."

"Too bad he already had a wife."

"You're a dick, Kimura, you know that?"

Cassius seemed to be only half tuned in, swirling the icy dregs in his tumbler. "It was totally selfish of them to spring it on me like that. The new grading system."

"You and eight hundred other people," the blond said.

Mason eyed the bowl of nuts. He wanted to move it aside, to reveal the envelope, but decided against it. It would be less likely to get pinned on him if someone else did.

Cassius waved dismissively, and gestured to Mason. "This guy got dressed up already. So what's your connection to the happy couple?"

"I'm a cousin of Martin's. On his mother's side."

"I've heard about her," he said, raising his eyebrows. "She's notorious."

Mason wanted to ask what he meant—whether she'd murdered someone, or had brazenly worn white after Labor Day, or just had strong opinions. Instead he reached for a handful of nuts as he spoke.

"You were all at college together, I take it. Where was that?"

Kimura responded. "A small prestigious liberal arts university. It's in upstate New York. You probably haven't heard of it."

"Kimura was the student body president," the blond said, looking at him rather than Mason. "That's probably why it's so exclusive these days. More than when we were there."

"You got elected to that position?" Mason said, eyeing Kimura.

He frowned. "In a landslide."

The voters must not have had to listen to him talk, Mason thought.

Reaching for the bowl of nuts, Kimura pulled it toward him to take a handful.

"I was an effective leader," he said. "Although

I don't remember all the details. There was a lot of molly around."

The others shared a laugh at that, and Mason smiled, forcing himself not to look at the lavender envelope, completely exposed now among the coasters and the napkins and the empty glasses. But Mason didn't need to point it out. One of the guys at the table who hadn't said much gestured to it.

"That looks like Martin's stationery."

Cassius reached for the envelope, and held it to his nose to sniff it, then read aloud: "For the hottie." He laughed. "Why would he have left this here?"

"Where did that come from?" the blond said, and waggled his fingers. "Hand it over."

Cassius frowned. "It's not for you."

"Of course it's for me. That's what Martin used to call me, back in the day."

Kimura guffawed. "It's not for you, son. I've been sitting at this table all evening. I was Martin's only true crush. He left it for me."

"You're both delusional," Cassius said, and scoffed, looking from one to the other. "I'm the apex hottie. It's an objective fact, and everyone knows it." He started to tear at the seal.

"Stop that," Kimura snapped, and stood up, slapping his hand. "It's not for you."

"So let's open it and find out, short stuff."

"Why would either one of you assume it's for you?" the blond said. He raised his voice. "I'm the hottie. Martin's words. Not mine."

"I can't believe the three of you all dated Martin," Mason said, "and still got invited to his wedding."

"'Dated' is a strong word," Kimura said, waving a hand. "It was a small town. There were very few suitable guys."

"A tiny selection of guys on our level," Cassius said. "Of course we all test-drove Martin."

"So how did Henry bag him?"

The blond frowned, and spoke slowly, as if Mason weren't very bright. "You know Henry is a lawyer, right? He's on a partner track at an aggressive law firm. That means he has a huge earning potential. There's nothing sexier than that."

"You know, you're the only person here who doesn't know us already," Kimura said. "What's your name, guy?"

"It's Mason."

"Mason here doesn't know any of us," Kimura said. "That means he can be objective." He snatched the envelope from Cassius and waggled it in the air.

"That's a great idea," the blond said, giving Mason the once-over. "He clearly knows nothing about fashion, so he can judge us on our hotness alone, not our style or our pasts."

"Fine," Cassius said flatly, and met Mason's gaze. "So tell us, cousin: which one of us is the hottie?"

"Oh, god," Mason mumbled, and eyed them in turn. "You all seem quite charming."

"It's not about charm," Cassius said. He unbuttoned his polo shirt, then pulled it off over his head, tossing the garment onto a table behind him. "Neither of you betas can compete with these pecs." The guy did have great musculature, and smooth skin. He flexed an arm. "Check this out."

"Impressive guns," Mason said, his brow furrowing as he watched him preen. Everyone was a little buzzed this late in the evening, with the freely flowing booze, but with that ego, Cassius probably would have pulled his shirt off stone sober.

"I don't have to take off my shirt," Kimura said. "Look at this bone structure. Twenty-four hundred years of Japanese nobility, descended from the sun goddess, distilled right here into physical perfection."

"That's quite a pedigree," Mason said. "You do have great skin."

"I could demonstrate what makes me the hottie," the blond said, and grabbed his crotch. "But I can't really do that in a public setting." The others laughed, and he added, "It's no joke. I've been blessed by nature."

"I'm not sure I need to see that," Mason said.

"Are you straight?"

"I'm not."

"So, what—you don't like big dicks?"

Mason held his gaze. "I'm just afraid that it'll make me sad, because no one else will ever live up to you."

The blond nodded, a pained look on his face. "I do hear that a lot."

"He's here," somebody said, and Mason turned to look.

It was Henry, striding in from the lobby. He was wearing jeans, and a sweatshirt with a team logo on it, and his hair was unkempt. He looked tired. In real life he was darker than his photo, Mason saw—the law firm had whitewashed him a little for its website.

"Cassius lost his shirt," Henry said, stepping up to the table, a grin on his face. "I'm sorry we didn't come by earlier. We just finished the rehearsal. Martin sends his regrets. He had to go for a Brazilian wax before tomorrow."

Slowly twisting sideways in his chair, Cassius put his forearm over the lavender envelope. The way he moved, and the fact that he was half naked, made it obvious that he was trying to look casual. It didn't work—he only drew more attention to what he was doing.

"What's this?" Henry said, and reached for

the envelope, pulling it out from under his arm.

"It's not what you think," Kimura said.

Henry read the front, and briefly held it to his nose, his brow furrowing. He ripped it open.

"That's actually for me," the blond said. "What does it say?"

Henry didn't respond as he folded open the sheet of notepaper and read it. His mouth tightened into a thin line, and he dropped the note on the table, then turned and walked out.

"Holy balls," Kimura said quietly. "What does it say?"

The blond read the note, then passed it to Cassius. "This means Henry knows that Martin is still carrying the torch for me—even at their wedding. I feel like a heartbreaker now."

Cassius pulled his shirt on. Once Kimura had read the note, he folded it and tossed it on another table. They were suddenly subdued, and sobered, the debate about the real hottie forgotten. Mason got up and walked into the lobby, then took the elevator up to his floor. His task had gone down the way Hanh had intended, the way they'd planned it, but he felt a pang of guilt. He wished he hadn't seen that look on Henry's face.

As he stepped off the elevator, he saw that the door to the first guest room was propped open by the security latch. It didn't have a room number, and instead bore a plaque that read PRESIDEN-TIAL SUITE. Inside he could hear heated voices. Glancing behind him to make sure he was alone in the hallway, Mason stepped closer and paused to listen.

Two men were arguing, although it was hard to make out the words. Then one of them got louder. It was Henry's voice: "You slut."

Mason kept walking, down the hall to his own room. In the myth, Paris had chosen the fairest, and had given the golden apple to Aphrodite. In this version no one got it, but somehow that little lavender envelope had managed to start a war.

Once he was undressed, he draped his suit over the lounge chair, then killed the lights and climbed under the covers. Feeling around for his phone on the night table, he called Ned.

"How's the wedding?" Ned said.

"I'm in bed already. The ceremony isn't until tomorrow."

"Did they have the out-of-towners reception tonight? You wouldn't have been asked to the rehearsal dinner."

"How do you know so much about wed-dings?" Mason demanded.

"They tend to follow a familiar pattern."

Mason told him about his day, and driving the absurdly large car, and Martin's competitive friends.

"You sound tired," Ned said.

"It's informative, though. If we ever do this, I know exactly what not to do."

Nine

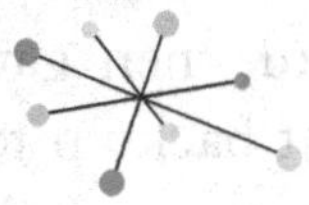

THE NEXT MORNING, MASON dressed in a plaid shirt and chinos, then went down to the lobby in search of coffee and breakfast. The buffet had java but not much for him to eat, and he made do with plain oatmeal and dry toast and a bruised banana.

As he walked out of the breakfast room into the lobby, he found a small crowd of people standing around the lounge furniture. Tanisha was among them, and waved him over when she spotted him.

"Have you heard?" she said, her tone hushed. She touched his forearm. "The ceremony is canceled."

"Really?" Mason frowned. "Why?"

"All I heard was that something irreconcilable came up between them. You know how lawyers are. That's likely as much as we'll get out of them. Still, I'd love to hear the juicy details."

"That's terrible news."

"Ray and I decided to head back to the city. Can I get your number? I'm sure I'll get out to California at some point."

Mason dug in his pants pocket and handed her a business card, then gave her an air kiss good-bye and went back up to his room. It was despicable, breaking up a couple, and the fact that it was his doing made his stomach queasy. How could this possibly be constructive?

At the little desk he pulled open his computer, and spent a minute looking for seats, and eventually got his flights rebooked for later today. After he'd had a shower, he got dressed and pulled on his backpack, and gathered his garment bag, and walked out to the elevator.

When the doors rolled open, the lone passenger was a woman in a flashy sari, in a deep red fabric run through by gold threads. On her forehead was a delicate red bhindi. It must be related to the third eye—the same point where he'd taped on the video cable the other day, although that fiasco had been decidedly less elegant than this woman's style.

"It looks like you're leaving," she said, eyeing Mason as he stepped on. This wasn't one of the relatives who'd come from India—her dialect was pure Northeast.

"I hear there's not going to be a wedding."

"We're having the party anyway, so as not to waste the alcohol and the food. Henry won't be here, of course." She leaned closer and spoke in a low tone, as if they might be overheard. "He took the honeymoon trip—with the wedding planner."

Mason's eyebrows shot up. "I did not see that coming." He wanted to ask if Henry had previously been romantically involved with the planner, but decided that would be too much.

"It's my family who's paying for all this," she said. "We don't want there to be any hard feelings. You should stay."

"Thank you for asking," Mason said, meeting her gaze, and as the doors rumbled open, he stepped off into the lobby.

He checked out at the reception desk, then carried his bags to the parking lot. It was still startlingly chilly and humid outside. As he approached his vehicle, it struck him as kind of amazing that the grass grew right up to the edge of the pavement—in this climate there was no bare earth anywhere.

Pressing the key fob, he stepped next to the vehicle to toss his bags in the backseat. A guy was leaning against the front fender, and he straightened up when Mason appeared, palming his cigarette and then turning his head to blow a puff of smoke. It was Martin, he realized. Mason had never seen him in person.

"Sorry," Martin said.

"Smoking doesn't bother me outside." Mason dropped his bags on the seat, then closed the door.

Martin dropped the cigarette to the asphalt and ground it under his shoe. "Then I'm sorry for leaning on your rig."

"It's not my car. I'm just using it for a couple more hours."

"Well, then, I'm sorry you're leaving. Sorry for everything." He looked away. "You're one of my mom's people, aren't you?"

Mason hesitated, but finally said, "That's right."

"I'm sorry she couldn't be here. Sorry it got called off."

"Things happen," Mason said. "It sounds like Henry's family is going to drink the booze and eat the food anyway."

Martin chuckled. "Did you hear he left with the wedding planner? I should have known. I saw a spark there."

"That must have been rough."

"It's my own fault. Not Henry's. I need to

learn to keep it in my pants." He met Mason's gaze. "You know what she's like. My mother, I mean. I'm just like her. I do stupid and destructive things. Are you like that?"

Mason shrugged. "I try to do the right thing. I know it's not always possible."

"Amen, brother."

"Do you need a ride? I'm headed west. Albany."

"I'm actually going to stay." He smiled. "I don't want all that food to go to waste."

He watched Martin walk back toward the lobby, then climbed in the car and got settled. With a deep breath to steel himself, he put it in gear, and eased out onto the street, and followed his phone's directions to the freeway. The trip back to Albany was calm, as the traffic wasn't as dense as it was in LA, and all the greenery took the edge off.

Once he'd turned in the car, and made it through security, and found a chair near his departure gate, he phoned Ned.

"I changed my flight," he said. "Can you pick me up tonight instead?"

"I can," Ned said, "although that doesn't give me much time to air out the cigar smoke and clean up after the go-go boys."

"Funny."

"Why are you coming home early?"

"The wedding was canceled," Mason said. "One of the grooms eloped with the wedding planner."

"Oh, my god, Mason—what is it with your family?"

"I'm boarding soon. I'll tell you all about it when I get home."

"Send me your itinerary."

After he'd transited at Philly, his seat on the long flight west was against the window, and he managed to sleep part of the way. When he couldn't anymore, he opened the saucer guy's religious book and had a closer read. It was hard to absorb, and felt rambling and scattered and disjointed, like wading through cheese dip, and eventually he had to give up.

When he got to the curb outside the terminal at LAX, he texted Ned his location, then phoned Hanh. The only number he had for her was the business line at Pretty Nail Blowout. The machine picked up.

"It's Mason," he said, "calling for Hanh. We need to talk."

Ned rolled up in the Barracuda, beaming at the sight of him, and climbed out to embrace him. He took the garment bag and Mason's backpack and tucked them into the trunk.

As they were climbing in, Ned glanced at him. "I want details."

Mason told him most of the story on the drive home, omitting his own role in it, and of course leaving out the part about the lavender envelope.

Ned braked to descend the ramp as he exited the freeway. "I can't figure out if it's just your family, or some Anglo thing, or a Protestant thing."

"Ask your mother if any of her people ever bailed on a wedding at the last minute. I bet it happens to Catholics too."

"You can ask her yourself, if you want. I'm going over to hang out with them tomorrow. After she gets back from mass."

"I think I'll need to sleep," Mason said. "But you should remind her how much I love her tamales."

Ned chuckled. "I'm sure she'll be happy to send you some more."

❧

Wiped out from the trip and the time change, Mason slept late, letting his body wake him. Once he'd caffeinated and had some fruit and muesli, he saw that he had a voice mail from Hanh.

"Drop by the shop today," was her terse message.

He got dressed and pulled on his backpack, then cycled down the hill and rode to Hollywood, relishing the dryness and the warmth of the air, so familiar and comfortable compared to the East, where the sky could crack open at any moment and inundate the landscape.

When he stepped into the nail salon, the receptionist smiled in greeting. "Miss Hanh is in the supply room."

Hanh was standing at the sink when he stepped into the back. She offered him a coffee, and poured one for herself too, and they both sat at the little table.

Mason sipped at the scalding acrid liquid and eyed the staffer who'd stepped in to grab a handful of towels. Once she'd gone back into the shop, he spoke.

"So I personally ruined the biggest day of someone's life. Two someones, in fact."

Hanh waved a hand. "The first wedding always feels like the most important. They'll both have other big days."

"What do I do with my guilt? I feel like a heel. An emotional thug."

"Guilt is a Western phenomenon. It acts as a corrosive, don't you find?"

He frowned. "Is there a non-Western alternative?"

"Why not just be embarrassed about what you did?"

"How is that better?"

"It takes the personal responsibility out of it.

You did something shady. That's embarrassing. So move on."

He considered that. "The way I rationalize it is that they had their own drama going on. Henry was already flirting with the wedding planner, and no one was surprised that Martin had been messing around on him. It didn't take much of a nudge to derail the ceremony."

"See? You're feeling better already—and your ego is intact."

"So what is it exactly that we prevented from happening?"

"It's too complicated to outline, but you should understand that you were successful. I knew you would be. You can be proud of that achievement."

Mason pursed his lips and watched her for a moment, cradling the warm mug in his hands. "So now it's payback time. I'm going to 1953."

Hanh laughed. "I expected no less. Have you considered why it is that you've been to the same point so many times? This city in that era."

"I didn't, actually. I thought the timing with Geraldine was just happenstance."

"Just a coincidence? There are no coincidences."

"I guess I know that."

She waved a hand. "So do you know the specific day you want to target?"

"Geraldine's trip is on a Friday," he said, and

told her the date. "I should go a day or so before that to get my bearings and make preparations."

"When do you want to start?"

"I'm basically ready."

"So let's say after business hours this evening."

Mason nodded. "I assume we'll need a third psychic again to summon sufficient energy?"

"I think not. I should be able to get you there myself."

He frowned. "What's changed since last time?"

"You've been there twice already."

"That makes it easier?"

"You're beating a path to that point," she said. "Think of the first time you wear flip-flops in the summer. Your toes feel them all day, but then they get used to it. By the third day you don't even notice."

"OK." Maybe he did need to think about why he kept going back there. "So where will we do this?"

"That's up to you. You'll have to depart and return in the same spot for me to be able to find you."

"My target actually lives not far from this part of town," Mason said. "We could do it here, in your alley."

"That's easy for me." She raised her eyebrows. "First you should make sure this alley wasn't something else in 1953. The middle of a warehouse, or a cement silo, or a train depot."

He frowned. "Can't you check?"

"It's your undertaking. You can do the work." She rose and reached for his mug.

"I guess I'll figure it out." Mason pulled on his backpack. "See you this evening." As he made his way back through the shop, and walked out, he couldn't help but smile. Hanh was going to keep her end of the deal—this was really happening.

He retrieved his bicycle and cycled to the metro, cruising fast with newfound energy, then rode downtown. Once he'd climbed up the stairs out of the ground, he cycled to the central library, and locked his ride to the bicycle rack out front, and went inside.

Maps and street plans were downstairs, next to the history department. Harmony wasn't on the desk, he saw. Maybe Sunday was her day off. Once he'd found the historic maps of the city, he compared several versions dating from around that time, and finally decided the alley behind Hanh's shop had been an alley even in the 1950s. It didn't mean that he wouldn't arrive in the middle of a smaller obstacle, a car or a fence or a trash can, but hopefully she had some way to help him avoid that.

Shelved nearby were city directories through the years, and he found the one for 1953, and looked up Billy's phone number. It had his address as well, and he wrote both on his note-pad. Billy was a guy he'd hired to help him out last time, and as they'd worked together, they'd built a rapport. With any luck the directory was accurate. The only other way he had to track the guy down was to look for him at the clandestine gay bar where they'd first met, but that could take more time than he had—there was no guarantee he'd be there on any given evening.

He couldn't take the note with him, he decided. He'd have to commit the details to memory. Geraldine's home address had been in one of the newspaper articles, and he pulled out his laptop to find it again, then studied an online map of her location and Billy's, working to memorize all the numbers and the nearest cross-streets.

Some of the stuff in the article might be useful, he realized, and he reread the part about how the sheriff's deputies had found Geraldine's car in the desert. Once he'd finished, he went through the phone number and addresses once again in his head, until he was confident that he'd stored them.

Packing up his stuff, he walked up to the street, and unlocked his bicycle to ride the few blocks to his office. The building was quiet on the weekend, and when he wheeled his ride into his space, he saw the VCR still sitting on his desk, wires dangling from it. That seemed so long ago now. He'd donate the machine back to the thrift store, he decided. He hadn't even pulled off the piece of masking tape that said FUNCIONA.

Buried in his filing cabinet was a folder labeled 1950s, and he went over and pulled it out. In an unsealed envelope was his antique cash, purchased from a currency dealer the last time he'd done this. None of the bills were dated later than 1952. Counting it, there was over three hundred dollars. Money stretched a lot farther back then—this should be enough for a few days.

Stuffing it into his pants pocket, he dumped the vintage coins out of the envelope and pocketed them as well, along with the other stuff he'd acquired for that era: his membership card to the Blue Moon club, and his 1952 District of Columbia driver's license. It bore a black-and-white headshot of him with a blank expression on his face.

Wheeling his bicycle to the elevator, he went down to the lobby, and across the street, and down the stairs to the metro. When he got home, sweating from pedaling uphill on the last stretch, he saw that Peggy was outside on the balcony. Her computer was open on her lap, and she was wearing a sweater—it wasn't very warm out, although it got sunny there in the afternoon.

Mason made a pot of espresso and poured a

demitasse cup for himself, and one for her, then found the peeler and cut a strip of rind from a lemon in the fruit bowl, and set it on the saucer. He usually didn't bother with it for himself, but he knew she liked to spritz it in her espresso.

"Can I interrupt?" he said, as he stepped outside and set one of the cups on the table next to her.

She folded her computer closed and smiled at the sight of the java. "You know what I like. How was the wedding?"

"It got canceled the night before." He dropped into the other chair and sipped at his cup.

"Oh, the drama—I love it."

Mason told her the broad strokes of what had happened.

As she sipped from the little cup, her brow furrowed. "You said before that you were supposed to stir things up. Did that include getting the whole thing canceled?"

He shrugged. "It was Hanh's ask."

"That woman is so bizarre."

"I think it was meant to change the course of things. To prevent something negative from happening."

"Do you have any idea what?"

"She didn't explain it. But she said they'd both find other relationships."

"And that makes it OK?" Peggy demanded.

"I have to assume it mitigates my actions."

He gestured helplessly and looked away, surveying their hilly neighborhood and the boulevard below. Peggy picked up the lemon peel and spritzed the last of it into her cup.

"Listen," he said. "Can I access your design skills again?"

"Are you going to bust up another wedding?"

Mason winced at that. "I need a basic business card that won't look like an anachronism in 1953. I'm going after Geraldine tonight."

She drained her cup and rose. "Let's do it."

In her room, Peggy sat at her computer, and Mason told her what details he wanted to include on the card. She soon came up with a simple design, and printed six of them on a sheet of cardstock. Next she cut them to size with a hobby knife and a ruler.

MASON BRAITHWAITE
PRIMAVERA BUILDING · LOS ANGELES
INVESTIGATIONS

"They're freaking perfect," Mason said, admiring one and then shuffling them into a stack.

"What was in your building in 1953?"

"I think it was still that insurance company. Nobody's going to be looking for me there, though. I just need these to sell a story."

In the bedroom he grabbed his suit pants, then went to the dining table and spread them

147

out. Inside the top hem, under the belt loops, there were several hidden pockets, designed as a hiding place. The thinking was that if he got mugged, it was unlikely he'd lose his pants. He separated the period cash into piles by denomination, then folded most of the twenties into the hidden recesses, and tucked the smaller bills into the front pocket, along with the old coins.

Next he spent time in the bathroom with his razor to get a thorough close shave, then got dressed, in the vintage shirt and the hibiscus-print tie, knotting it to hang short, the way guys wore them back then. Once he'd pulled on the derbies that came with the suit he checked his look in the floor mirror. Nothing would be out of place where he was going.

More than anyone he looked like Buster, the gritty protagonist from a series of 1940s films that he'd watched with Ned. Even though Buster was a bit of a pugilist, he was a great role model for the social behavior and the language people used back then. Pulling his fedora on and adjusting it low over his brow, he studied his reflection, and then channeled Buster, in a flat voice: "Looking good, toots."

No way was he going to ride his bicycle in this getup. He called a ride-share, then pocketed a lone modern-day fin to tip the driver with. Compared to the dark-green antique cash, it looked positively purple, the portrait of Honest Abe lurid in its current oversize unframed rendering. Putting his phone on silent, he left it in the nightstand drawer with his keys.

On the way out, he stopped in Peggy's doorway.

"If Ned asks, I have a psychic thing tonight."

"He's still with his family?" As she turned to look, her eyes grew wide. "Wow—you're actually doing this."

"I hope so."

"You lead a very strange life." She got up to give him a hug. "Good luck."

He went out to the driveway to wait for his ride. Climbing in, he felt naked not having his phone with him, like he was missing something. The driver wasn't chatty, and without a screen to look at, Mason sat in silence and watched the dark city roll by.

Hanh's shop was just a few minutes' ride, and as he climbed out in the parking lot, he remembered to hand the guy the fin.

The shop was closed for the evening, and dark inside. He rapped on the glass door with a knuckle. A moment later Hanh appeared, and flipped the deadbolt to let him in.

"You look ready," she said, stepping aside.

"I think so."

After she'd locked the door again, she led him

through the darkened salon to the back room.

"Just a reminder," she said. "Don't change anything beyond the bare minimum of your task."

"That's a bad idea, I take it."

"You already know that."

"Somehow I think what I'm doing can't be all that bad," Mason said, "or you wouldn't have gone along with it."

Her eyes narrowed. "What you're doing is unusual. Very few people ever develop the ability, or manage to focus it so precisely. With this power comes the burden of acting responsibly."

"I understand," he said, holding her gaze.

Hanh turned and heaved on the fire door, pushing her way outside. As they stepped into the middle of the alley, she glanced around. Pools of light illuminated the ground outside the back doors lining the alley, but no one was in view.

"You remember the drill," she said quietly. "Crouch slightly, on your toes, and I'll shove you into the target time frame."

"You remember the date?"

"I know what I'm doing, Mason. You have to help. Focus your energy on me."

He felt a sudden twinge of nerves, and took a breath. "Remind me how I get back."

"Come to the alley again and do the same thing—focus your energy, and I'll pull you back here. Make sure you're in the same spot."

Mason adjusted his hat, lower and tighter on his head, then tugged up on his pant legs as he leaned forward, balanced on his toes. Closing his eyes, he took a minute to focus his energy, envisioning a white ball of light in his chest, and then visualized it arcing into Hanh.

"Ready," he mumbled, and opened his eyes a crack.

Hanh's expression had shifted, and her eyes were darker. It was almost like her face had different features now. Mason struggled to stay focused, not to succumb to his upwelling fear, to project his energy. Suddenly she lunged at him, shoving his chest, and he tumbled back, landing on his butt. In that moment Hanh blinked out of existence, and he was sitting alone on the gritty asphalt.

Ten

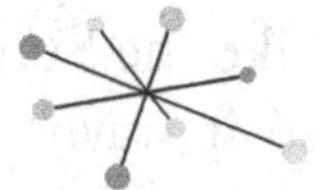

RIGHT AWAY IT WAS obvious that Mason was somewhere different. There was still light in the sky, and the air was warmer, and it felt muggy. Rising, he slapped the dust off his butt and took a deep breath.

Landmarks, he remembered. He'd need land-marks to get aligned for his return trip. Right where he'd fallen, there was a kidney-shaped pothole. That seemed pretty distinctive. Eyeing the buildings on either side, he mentally stored the position he was in so that he could find it again: next to the second post in the chain-link fence, just past the steel door with DELIVERIES painted in big black letters.

"Where did you come from?"

It was a man's voice, and Mason spun around to face him. Sitting on the asphalt in the shadows next to the fence, he had a week's worth of whiskers, and a stained and shabby jacket. Dangling from the hand that was propped on his knee was a bottle in a brown paper bag. His eyes were wide.

"Just passing through," Mason said, and turned on his heel, and made his way out onto Sunset.

It felt nothing like the Sunset he knew. Twilight was fading, so it wasn't that late, but the boulevard felt abandoned, as if it were well into the night. There was no nightlife around here, it seemed, just darkened shops, and the sidewalk felt poorly lit compared to his own version of this place.

He stopped at the curb to watch the passing vehicles, the hulking noisy cars driving by. Lumbering old machines, they were, and he focused on the sound of them, the colors and the movement, working to get mentally grounded. This wasn't just about looking around—he was really here, body and all. Breathing deeply, he could feel the place settling in, becoming fully solid— or maybe it was more about him becoming solid in this place.

There was an odd smell, he realized, the tang of something noxious. Diesel soot, maybe, and definitely ozone. A humpback car drove by. Even in the low light he could see it was a surreal shade of powder blue.

It was Wednesday evening. That gave him thirty-six hours or so before Geraldine drove out to the desert. He walked west, assuming his rapid commuter pace, feeling a bit of urgency now. His plan was to ask Billy for help, but first he needed to track him down.

At the end of the block he found a phone booth, and stepped inside, and picked up the receiver. There was a solid buzzy tone when he held it to his ear, so he cranked in Billy's number on the rotary dial. Nothing happened—he could still hear the tone. What was he doing wrong?

On the sidewalk, a guy strolled past the booth, dressed the same way Mason was, with a broad hat low over his eyes. Should he ask him how the thing worked? It would seem pretty stupid not to know how to use a pay phone.

Hanging up the receiver, he huffed in frustration. He'd only been here a few minutes and already he was stuck. Overconfidence had never been a problem for Mason, but right now he suddenly felt like a tyro, like showing up here unprepared might be his downfall.

There was a plaque on the front of the phone's housing, he saw, next to the receiver, and it actually bore a list of instructions. The first line said

INSERT COINS. Maybe that was the procedure—cash up front.

Digging in his pocket, he found a dime and dropped it into the slot. It fell through into the little tray at the bottom. He picked up the receiver and tried it again, and this time the line clicked and the coin stayed inside. As he started to dial Billy's number again, the dial tone stopped. One he'd cranked in all the numbers, it started to ring. But there was no answer, and no voice mail software to intercede, and eventually he hung up. His coin dropped into the tray, and he scooped it out and pocketed it. Unanswered calls must be no charge. He folded his arms and stared at the device. He should have had a backup plan.

Behind him came a sharp *tap-tap* on the glass of the booth's door. A woman was standing there, wearing a little hat and a long coat despite the warm evening, scowling at him.

"Are you finished in there?" she said.

Mason stepped out and held the door for her, then looked around the street. He wasn't helpless here, he reminded himself. Just a little underprepared. He had cash in his pocket, and that meant he could do stuff.

The neighborhood felt a little seedy, partly because of the wan street lighting, and partly because there weren't a lot of people around. Setting off, he walked west, glancing into the shop windows as he went. He could go to the Blue Moon, he decided, before he got a place to sleep. If Billy wasn't around, maybe he could find someone else with local knowledge.

But it was too early for a bar, so he crossed Sunset and strolled deeper into Hollywood, soaking up the bygone atmosphere. It was still a factory, he realized, walking the deserted streets. With no high-rises or shops or eateries, the buildings were all industrial—a sound studio, a film vendor, a camera lens place. In his time all these businesses had moved to roomier spaces in newer neighborhoods.

A while later, when his feet were starting to tire, he decided it was late enough for the Blue Moon. The club was downtown, and to get there he'd have to figure out where the streetcar line was. He'd need to ask someone about that.

There was a better chance of finding people on the boulevard, and he headed back to Sunset. Before he came across anyone, another phone booth appeared, and he stepped inside. This time, on the third ring, a familiar voice answered.

"I'm so glad you picked up. It's Mason—remember me?"

"Hey, buddy," Billy said, his tone rising. "How are you? Are you in town?"

"I just got in. I'd like to see you. Do you have some time tomorrow?"

"Where are you staying?"

"I'm in Hollywood right now."

"That's where I live," Billy said. "Why don't you come over this evening?"

As he rattled off his address, Mason heaved a sigh of relief. He already knew where Billy's place was, memorized from that long-ago phone book. From here it would be less than half an hour's walk.

Making his way out of the industrial part of the neighborhood, he took the back streets and ogled the houses. Some were structures he'd seen, or their close predecessors, but many were totally unfamiliar—a whole block of tall wooden Victorians, clad in narrow board siding, painted white with dark shingles. Mature shade trees lined the sidewalk. He'd never seen anything like this. It had been replaced with more density, with those ubiquitous squat apartment buildings.

Billy's neighborhood was mostly detached houses and a few small apartments. Walking up on his address, he saw that it was a two-story house on a corner. This was definitely the right place—parked in the driveway was Billy's cute little yellow pickup. Mason stepped up to the door and knocked.

When he pulled it open, Billy flashed a big smile. He wasn't very tall but he was buff, and had dark hair, and a prominent nose. He was wearing baggy pants and a shirt with several buttons open at the neck.

As Mason stepped in he gave him a brief hug.

"There's someone else here that you know," Billy said.

Standing back, near the bottom of the stairs, was Flattop. His real name was Eugene, but the nickname came from his distinctive blond brush cut. He was wearing a plaid shirt and pleated trousers. Mason didn't know him as well as Billy, but they'd done some work together.

Flattop beamed as Mason gave him a bro hug, and then Billy waved them into the kitchen, pulling a chair out from the table for him.

"Can I take your hat?" Billy said.

"I forgot I was wearing it." He pulled it off and tossed it on the kitchen counter.

"How about a beer?" Flattop said, stepping over to the fridge.

Billy sat at the end of the table. "Get him a glass."

"I don't need one," Mason said. "I'm not a fancy lad."

Billy's eyes narrowed. "Yes, you are. As I remember it, you didn't know the difference between a shovel and a shoehorn. You have the soft hands of a pianist."

"Or a banker," Flattop offered, handing each of them a dark brown bottle. As he sat between them, he briefly touched Billy's shoulder.

"I don't work with my hands," Mason said, "but I'm not a blue blood." He reached toward them to tap the neck of his bottle against each of theirs, then took a sip. "I'm getting the sense that you two are together."

"We are," Billy said, his eyes bright. "We moved in together a few months ago. This is a duplex—we bought the whole building and then put in a connecting door. It's basically one big house now, but with two kitchens and two baths."

"We're both on the deed," Flattop said, "but I tell people I'm his tenant. I park in front of the other unit. On the side street."

"That is so ingenious," Mason said. It meant they could be together privately and avoid the grinding homophobia of the time. Even more amazing was that their blue-collar incomes were enough to buy this house.

"You're one of the people who thought we should have an affair," Billy said, a wry grin on his face.

"If you're living together, it's obviously more than that."

Flattop blushed and drank from his bottle.

"I hate that you have to hide your relationship," Mason said.

Billy frowned. "That's for self-preservation.

We could get arrested if people knew we were sleeping together. At the very least we'd get our heads busted open. I can't believe it doesn't work that way where you live."

"You're from back east, right?" Flattop said.

"I'm sure it's the same there." Mason flashed a palm. "You know I'm a little clueless sometimes."

Billy nodded. "So what brings you back to town?"

"Work. I wanted to hire one of you, or maybe someone you know, for a job."

"Burying stuff in a stranger's backyard again?" Flattop said.

Mason had to laugh. "Nothing quite so risky."

"Maybe he needs to dig it up now," Billy said. "That glass sculpture."

"The Melted Pineapple can stay where it is. I just need a ride back to town."

"From where?"

"Out in the Mojave. Friday afternoon."

"Unfortunately I have to work," Billy said.

"I have a vehicle." Flattop gestured with his bottle. "Maybe I could take the day off and drive out."

"It's far," Mason said, "and it's for a job, so I'll pay you for your time, and gas, and wear and tear."

"You don't need to pay me for a ride."

"He's on a job," Billy said, eyeing him. "That means his client is paying."

"In that case," Flattop said, "I'll take your client's money. The Mojave is pretty big. Where will you be, exactly?"

"It's a place called Giant Rock," Mason said. "Kind of between Victorville and Twentynine Palms. You get there via the Gorgonio Pass. It's about fifteen miles off the main road."

"Isn't there an airstrip at Giant Rock?" Flattop said, his brow furrowing.

"I think it's just a salt pan where they cleared the rocks so you can land a plane. There's no gas or anything."

"Oh, Mason," Billy said. "You're about to make a friend for life."

Mason eyed him. "Explain."

Flattop wrapped his hands around his bottle. "Toward the end of the war I was in pilot training. I got my papers, but V Day came before I got deployed overseas."

"Lucky for you," Mason said. "Lots of people never came back."

He nodded. "Civilian aviation is a rich man's game. I never get the chance to fly."

"You're thinking you'll pick me up at Giant Rock in an airplane."

"I'd have to rent one," he said, meeting his gaze. "It won't be cheap."

Mason remembered how Buster talked about money, and ran through the euphemisms he used.

"What kind of lettuce are we talking about?"

Flattop didn't even blink at the word. "For the day, one twenty, plus maybe another thirty for fuel and incidentals."

"So one fifty total?" Mason nodded. "I can do that."

A broad smile spread across his face. "Let me get on the horn to see if I can arrange it. What time do you want me to be there?"

"I'm not sure, exactly. I'd hate to make you wait around in the summer heat in the middle of nowhere. Late afternoon?"

"As long as we can get back by dark, it's not a problem."

Flattop rose and went into the front room, and a moment later Mason heard the distinctive mechanical whir of the dial on a rotary phone.

"You two are adorable together," he said, eyeing Billy.

His face went red. "Aw, shucks, Mason." He took a swig of beer. "I will say, it feels right. Are you still with the same guy?"

"I am. He thinks my job is crazy, but other than that, we get along."

When Flattop came back, he sat down with them again. "I got us a 120 for the day."

"What's a 120?" Mason said.

"It's the kind of airplane. Single prop, tail dragger, room for two."

"Is it safe?"

"Safer than a car." He raised his eyebrows. "There's nothing to bump into up there."

"Except the ground."

Flattop waved dismissively. "It only goes a hundred miles an hour at top speed. Even if the engine conks out, you just glide back to earth. You can land one of those anywhere."

"Let's plan that the engine won't fail," Mason said.

"If you want, I can fly you out there, and come back later to pick you up. It won't cost you any more."

"I have the outbound trip set up already," Mason said. That wasn't at all true, but he had to be on the ground, close to Geraldine. He wasn't sure yet how he was going to make that happen. "Can I use your bathroom?"

"Top of the stairs," Billy said, waving to the front room.

When he stepped into it, the space felt compact, designed in a much less self-indulgent time to accomplish the necessities, not for lounging and pampering. Folding the seat down, he loosened his belt and sat, then worked the cash out of the little pockets in the top hem of his pants, counting out a hundred and fifty bucks.

Back in the kitchen, he set the bills on the table. "Here's the lettuce."

Billy frowned as he eyed the pile. "Did you rob a bank?"

Flattop scooped it up and quickly counted it, then nodded. "Let's do some flying."

They clinked bottles again, and Mason sat back and took a swig of beer. His head was starting to hurt, likely from the time shift, and the new environment. But what a relief to be making headway, to have part of his excursion figured out. Thinking about it, though, there was a hitch—if anything went wrong with the rest of his plan, he'd have no way to alert Flattop.

"You know, there's a chance that I won't make it out there," Mason said.

Flattop frowned. "I already booked the plane."

"That's fine—I'm not going to back out. But I won't know until Friday whether I'm able to get all the way there or not. When you come to pick me up at Giant Rock, if you can't find me, don't wait. Just fly home again before it gets dark."

"I get it," Flattop said. "Sundown is just before eight, so I have to be in the air again by six at the latest. Are you driving out there? What are the odds that you'll make it?"

"I plan on being there, but I still have some of the details to sort out. If everything holds together, I'd say eighty percent."

"God willing and the creek don't rise," Billy said, and grinned.

Mason frowned. "There's a creek?"

"It's just an expression. About unforeseen circumstances."

"That's exactly where I'm at."

"You look tired," Billy said.

"I've had quite a day." Mason rubbed his eyes.

"Where are you staying?"

"I'm going to get a room at the Baltimore."

"You really are a fancy fellow," Flattop said.

"Why not stay here?" Billy waved an arm. "You can have a whole bedroom all to yourself. Completely befitting a blue blood."

"We sleep in my place," Flattop said.

Mason eyed them in turn. "You're sure it's no imposition?"

"Nobody sleeps in Billy's bed."

"All the action happens in yours, huh," Mason said.

Flattop blushed. "The light is better there in the morning."

"You guys are making my life so easy."

"We girls have to stick together," Billy said, raising his eyebrows.

"Are you still doing drag?"

"Mamie gets to go out once in a while," he said, "although Eugene isn't a big fan."

"Let's say I tolerate her," Flattop said.

"Dressing up like Mamie makes me feel invincible."

Flattop scoffed. "That'll change when you get arrested."

"I get it," Mason said. "It's empowering."

Flattop eyed him. "Do you wear dresses too?"

"I don't think I could pull it off. I'd look like an orangutan trying to ride a unicycle."

"You're too tall, and too thick. You'd definitely get arrested."

"I have to be up early," Billy said. "Time for shut-eye. Let me get you a towel."

Mason rose and followed him into the front room.

"That's the other apartment," Billy said, gesturing through an open doorway next to the stairs. The lights were on, and the room looked similar to this one.

"You put in the doorway yourself?"

"I wasn't about to pay a carpenter to do it."

Mason followed him upstairs. The bedroom was small but comfortable, with flowery drapes in a riot of color.

"Do you want me to wake you when I get up?" Billy said, handing him a towel.

"That would be great."

Billy said good-night, and Mason got undressed, draping his suit over the chair in the corner. Sleep overcame him almost as soon as he'd crawled into the sheets.

Eleven

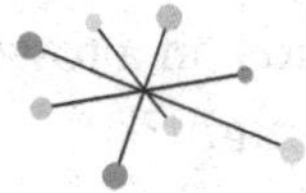

F ROM THE LIGHT OUTSIDE it looked like the sun was up, just barely, when Mason heard a knock at the bedroom door. It swung open to reveal Flattop, dressed in his green gas-company coveralls, with EUGENE embroidered on a patch on his breast.

"Rise and shine," he said.

"Are you kidding me right now?" Mason demanded, and forced himself to sit up.

Flattop laughed and stepped out. Mason heard him call down the stairs: "Somebody's not a morning person."

Once he'd washed up, and got dressed, he

went down. Flattop was gone, but Billy was in the kitchen, dressed in jeans and a heavy work shirt, rinsing a bowl in the sink.

"I remember you like fruit."

"You don't have to feed me too," Mason said.

"There's some oranges and apples in the icebox. Help yourself. I have to get to work."

"Thank you," Mason said. He could smell coffee—it must be in the pot on the stove.

"If you're going out of town on Friday," Billy said, drying his hands on a towel, "does that mean you'll stay another night?"

"Would you mind?"

"Of course not." He dug in his front pocket and handed Mason a key. "Just lock up when you leave. Come back whenever you want. We both get home after six."

"Thank you for trusting me, Billy. It means a lot."

"I know you, pal. You're not a crook." He shrugged. "Plus last night you took Flattop at his word, and handed him more money than I see in a week. The trust goes both ways."

Once he'd left, Mason poured himself a mugful of coffee from the tin pot on the stove. It was a percolator, he realized, with a little glass bubble in the top of the lid. The java was lukewarm but surprisingly good, and strong, the way he liked it.

In the fridge he found the promised fruit, and

ate some, sipping the joe as he gradually woke up. Geraldine lived in Koreatown, he knew, and that was walkable from here. It would be easier than asking someone what bus to take, and where the stop was, and figuring out how it all worked, like he'd just fallen off the turnip truck.

It was warm today, he found, stepping out the front door. He paused to lock it, pocketing Billy's key, and then strode out to the sidewalk. Across the street he saw a guy climbing into a car, wearing a suit like his, and a broad-brimmed hat. His hat—he'd forgotten it.

Turing on his heel, he went back into the house and found the fedora hanging on the rack near the front door. It wasn't where he'd put it last night, but this was definitely where he should have left it.

Back outside, he noticed that smell again, the tang of ozone hanging in the air. But otherwise it was a beautiful sunny morning. As he made his way up the block, a woman smiled at him as they passed.

This really was a different world. In the daylight the cars were even more striking, some in rich dark colors, others in pastels. In the side yards between the houses were clotheslines strung with laundry.

As he got into the neighborhood where Geraldine lived, it felt denser, with apartment buildings lining the streets. Walking up her block, his heartbeat quickened—was that her car? It was parked in front of her address. The dark-red color was right, and as he got closer, he saw the branding inscribed in chrome on the trunk: PACKARD 200. That matched the vehicle the sheriff's deputies had found.

The building was small, a dozen units on two floors around a narrow leafy courtyard. There was no front gate, nothing to stop him from walking in and knocking on Geraldine's door. But was that too forward? He hadn't really thought this part through, how exactly he was going to approach her. Not a door knock, he decided. She would come outside eventually.

Strolling to the end of the block, he realized there was nowhere he could loiter to stake out her building. Maybe he did need to come up with a reason to knock. But what was he going to say?

Farther up the block a gardener was mowing a lawn. He could smell the freshly cut grass. Crossing the street, he walked back on the other side, hands in his pockets.

He caught sight of someone walking out of Geraldine's courtyard. A woman, with dark hair and sunglasses, wearing a sleeveless white top and capri pants. Her age was about right, but he'd never actually seen a photo of Geraldine—the newspaper articles hadn't included one, and he hadn't managed to track one down. In one hand she carried a wooden box by a handle on the top. It had mesh panels on the sides. A cat carrier, he realized—that was Sylvester.

Opening the passenger door of the dark-red sedan, she loaded the box on the front seat, then stepped around and got in behind the wheel.

"Damn it," he muttered, watching her pull into the street and drive away. He hadn't even had time to think about approaching her.

The newspaper article said that Geraldine had left her cat with Margaret for the weekend— that must be where she was going now. It also said that Margaret lived down in Gramercy Park. It would take at least an hour for Geraldine to get there and back.

Mason walked the few blocks to Western Avenue, then strolled the retail storefronts until he found a diner. It looked quiet. He stepped inside and sat at the counter. The waitress had the distinctive wrinkles of a heavy smoker and wore a blue-and-white uniform with a little hat pinned in her gray hair.

"Are you planning to stay?" she said, stepping over.

"Can I see a menu?"

She nodded to the entrance. "Once you've hung your hat."

He'd forgotten about it, and got up long

enough to pull it off and hang it on the rack by the door.

"Just bring me a coffee," he told her, "and plain oatmeal without the fixings, and a fruit cup."

She wrote it on her little pad with a stubby pencil and stepped away. Glancing around, he saw there were two guys in laborer's clothes at a table in the corner, eating in silence, and a guy in a suit on his own by the window, studying a folded-up newspaper, but otherwise the place was empty.

The coffee was thin like tea—he could see the bottom of the cup. That meant there was next to no caffeine in it, which would only make his headache worse. The fruit came in a little parfait glass and must have come from a can, as it was mushy and packed in sickly sweet syrup, with halved maraschino cherries. The oatmeal was gooey and salty, but at least it tasted like oatmeal.

When he was almost finished the waitress tore off his check and set it in front of him. He watched her step away, feeling full but not at all sated by the grub. He really was out of place here. Pulling out his cash, he left a single and some coins, then got up to leave, and grabbed his hat from the rack by the door. Stepping out into the sunlight, he pulled it on, and took a breath, and headed back toward Geraldine's apartment.

As he rounded the corner on her block, he

saw a guy in dark work clothes sweeping the front walk, methodically making his way from the courtyard toward the street. His hair was thinning, and he was a little chubby. Mason considered whether he should talk to him, but as he got closer, the guy made the decision for him—he stopped sweeping and straightened up to look at him.

"Good morning," Mason said, and stopped.

His brow furrowed. "Are you here about the room to rent?"

He lifted his hat, shifting it higher on his head. "Can I see it?"

"Follow me." He walked to the outdoor staircase that led up to the second floor and propped the broom against the railing. "My name is Parker. I'm the super."

Mason told him his name as he followed him up the stairs.

"This place will go quickly," Parker said, glancing over his shoulder. "There's still a housing shortage."

The upstairs walkway was open-air as well, and Parker led him to the turquoise-blue door marked 202. Mason glanced across the courtyard at the other wing of the building. Geraldine's apartment was 206—it must be right over there.

Producing a ring of keys, Parker soon had the door open, and stood aside for Mason to enter.

He walked around, giving the hardwood floors a perfunctory glance. There was greenery outside the bedroom window, and the kitchenette had pink tile and a squat bulky stove. Above the kitchen sink, the window looked out at the walkway and the courtyard.

"It's nice," Mason said, returning to the front door. "But I don't think it'll be big enough."

"You need room for the wife and kids?"

"That's the story."

"Well, if you change your mind, I'm in 101, under the stairs."

"Is it OK if I look around the building?" he said, and stepped outside.

"There's not much to it, but knock yourself out," Parker said, locking the door. "No skin off my nose."

He watched Parker start to lumber down the stairs, then walked in the other direction, farther along the walkway, past the other apartments. Glancing down at the courtyard he saw Parker take his broom and disappear beneath his feet.

If all the apartments were like the one he'd just been in, the kitchen windows faced this walkway. Geraldine's apartment had the curtains drawn, and he stopped in front of it for a moment. There was nothing to see except the front door, painted turquoise like they all were. He put his hands on his hips, considering his next move.

Then the curtains snapped open, and a woman stood there at the kitchen sink, scowling at him. Mason held up a hand in greeting, then quickly walked toward the stairs and down into the courtyard, feeling his face heating up.

A roommate, maybe, or one of Geraldine's relatives. The newspaper stories hadn't mentioned her. He walked as calmly as he could—there was no reason to flee. She didn't come out to confront him, and soon he was down in the courtyard, out of her line of sight.

Walking out to the street, he saw the familiar dark-red car pull up. This was fortuitous timing—synchronicity. Taking a deep breath, he stood on the sidewalk and waited for Geraldine to park. He took a deep breath to steady himself as she got out and stepped around to the curb.

"Are you Miss Reed?" Mason said.

She paused and pushed her sunglasses up into her hair, looking him over. "That's right."

Mason smiled and pulled his hat off, the way Buster did when he talked to dames. "My name is Mason. I'm new in the neighborhood, and I was talking to Parker. He mentioned that you were going out to the Mojave this weekend."

Her eyebrows shot up. "I don't remember telling Mr. Parker about that."

"Maybe he overheard you talking to someone else." Mason leaned toward her and lowered his voice. "He does seem a little nosy."

"Well, I guess that's part of his job."

"I need to get to Twentynine Palms. I thought maybe we could share expenses on the trip."

"I'm not going to Twentynine Palms."

"That's fine," Mason said, and waved his hat. "I could ride part of the way with you, and get another ride after."

Geraldine frowned, and studied his face. "You're not a masher, are you?"

Mason wasn't sure what that meant, exactly, so he said, "I'm just a guy who needs a lift." He dug out a business card and handed it over, along with his D.C. driver's license.

"You're a long way from home."

"I'll be living here soon, but I haven't got a California ID yet."

Geraldine handed the license back, but held on to the card. "Are you working out at Twentynine Palms?"

"Doing some research. I'm an investigator."

"Are you packing a heater?"

"I'm not actually a private investigator. I can't really talk about the case I'm on, but it won't involve any violence, and I'm not armed."

She eyed his business card again. "The Primavera Building. That's an insurance company. Don't they provide you with a car?"

"Not until next week. You know what the

bureaucracy is like in a big organization. Stacks of paperwork. But I need to do an interview out there this weekend." Mason waved his hat. "I know I could rent a car, but I don't enjoy driving. When I heard about you, I thought, why not team up?"

"I don't know," she said, and folded her arms. "It's a long trip."

"If you get sick of my face, you can leave me on the side of the road. No hard feelings. I'll hitch another ride."

She watched him for a moment. "It might not be such a bad thing to have a man in the car. Can you change a flat?"

"Blindfolded, and with one hand tied behind my back." It was a brazen lie, but hopefully he wouldn't be tested on it.

"If I provide the vehicle, would you buy the gas? I mean all of it. For the whole trip out."

"Gladly," he said, and grinned.

"Do you have cash for that? I can't be taking your checks."

"I'll bring cash."

Geraldine nodded. "OK. But it's my vehicle, so no backseat driving. And you'll stay on your side of the car, and keep your hands to yourself." She raised her eyebrows. "No monkey business."

"On my honor," Mason said, and held up a palm.

She scoffed. "I'm leaving at sunup. You'll have to be here at five-thirty."

"I can do that."

"Well—I guess I'll see you then, Mr. Braithwaite."

"You can just call me Mason."

"And you can call me Geraldine." She stepped past him, headed into the building.

Walking up the block, his steps felt lighter, and he smiled to himself. It had worked—what a relief. His backup plan had been vague, to rent a car and try to follow her tomorrow, but that would have been so much more effort, with the constant risk that he'd lose track of her. This was by far the optimal path. Now he just had to make the rest of it work.

❧

WHEN HE GOT BACK to Billy and Flattop's neighborhood, he knew there had to be a market somewhere nearby. He couldn't just look for one on his phone, he remembered, absently digging for it in his pants pocket. Not for half a century at least. He walked along the boulevard, and scanned the storefronts, and within a couple of blocks he found a grocer.

Inside he was struck by the smells—spices, and fruit, and greens. He'd never seen a shop with board floors before, and he wandered the aisles, ogling the offerings, taking it all in. Eventually he found a display of mineral water. A fresh-faced kid of high-school age, wearing an apron and a bow tie, walked past, and Mason hailed him.

"Can I get two boxes of these?"

"There's six in a case. You want twelve bottles?"

"That would be great."

"Yes, sir. I'll take them to the register for you."

There was a lot of canned food for sale, he saw, strolling toward the back. No way was he going to mess with that, not after that syrupy diner fruit. Instead he picked up a box of saltines and a bag of apples.

At the front a middle-aged guy rang him up, deftly punching the mechanical buttons on an old-school cash register.

"The water is mine too," Mason said.

He eyed the boxes on the floor and nodded.

"You know, I hadn't thought about how I'm going to get those home."

"We can deliver them this afternoon," the guy said. "Seventy-five cents."

"Let's do that." Mason watched him bag the apples and the crackers, then paid him.

"Where are we making the delivery?"

"Right around the corner." Mason gave him Billy's address.

It was nice to walk out unencumbered, and he felt upbeat. Things were working out. He actually had time to kill now, before his hosts got home. More interesting than this neighborhood would be to go downtown. He spotted a woman waiting at a bus stop, and paused to talk to her.

"Can you tell me where the streetcar line is? The one that goes downtown."

"It runs on Santa Monica Boulevard," she said. "But the bus is right here."

Mason thanked her and walked toward Santa Monica. It was just a few minutes from here, and soon he was standing on the raised curb with a handful of other people, and boarded the crowded streetcar when it pulled up. When the conductor came by and eyed him, he knew what was expected, and he paid the fare in coins.

The car ran rough, and the steel wheels were loud. It took a while to get downtown. Somewhere around Echo Park or Westlake it entered a tunnel, and stayed underground right to the terminal under Hill Street.

Climbing up to the sidewalk, Mason walked past the Primavera Building. Stoic and beautiful, it looked the same, even the windows. Up the street he went into the central library. The layout was different, and this iteration was a much smaller building, but upstairs the atrium under the crowning pyramid was the same, with its lofty murals and bright chandelier.

Maybe this wasn't the best use of his time,

he realized. Gawking at things he already knew about was squandering an opportunity.

Outside again, he walked through Pershing Square. It looked like they were digging up part of it. There was a lot of construction noise around, and cranes overhead, with the city still in its post-war boom. Navigating the part of town he knew as Skid Row, he found it run-down, and parts of it were eerily similar to what he knew, the pawn brokers, cheap diners, parking lots. But the vibe was nowhere near as rough as in his day. That alone was remarkable, he realized—there was a complete absence of homeless encampments.

Eventually he went back to the terminal and boarded the streetcar back to Hollywood. It was still light out, but when he walked up on Billy's house, the yellow pickup was in the driveway. Digging out the key Billy had given him, he knocked on the door before he let himself in.

Billy was in the front room, lounging on the sofa, reading a newspaper by the light of a pole lamp.

"I got your grocery delivery," Billy said. "Are you planning on moving in?"

Mason chuckled as he pulled off his hat and hung it next to the door. "Those are for my road trip tomorrow. I actually have to get them to Koreatown."

Billy frowned. "Where, now?"

"Over by Western and Third." He stepped over and dropped into the lounge chair next to the sofa.

"There might be a Korean church around there," Billy said, "but I've never heard it called that."

He waved his arm. "I misspoke. My ride is over by that Korean church."

"You're an interesting fellow, Mason."

"Muddled, right? Maybe that's the best way to describe it." He rubbed his eyes.

"So you don't have a car, I take it. That's not far away—I can drop you and the groceries there in the morning. What time are you leaving?"

"I have to be there at five-thirty."

"So I'll wake you at five."

"I don't want you to have to get up early."

Billy grinned. "I'm up then anyway to get ready for work. Can I ask who you're riding with?"

"It's a long story. Do you have dinner plans? I want to take you guys out. To say thanks for letting me stay here."

"Fine by me," Billy said. "I'm sure Eugene will be up for it."

"Maybe Mexican? One of those places on Sunset."

"Dealer's choice. Eugene will be home soon."

"Call me when you're ready. I'm just going to rest my eyes."

Mason went upstairs and stretched out on the bed, not bothering to take off his shoes, letting his feet dangle over the side. He didn't plan on falling asleep, but soon Billy was there, his hand on his shoulder to wake him.

"How long was I out?" he mumbled, sitting up.

"About forty winks."

Downstairs the three of them piled into Billy's little pickup, with Eugene in the middle, straddling the gearshift, completely unself-conscious about being crowded so close together. Billy drove up to Sunset and parked behind the restaurant, and they went inside and got a booth.

The place was familiar from his own visits here, with the same wrought-iron decor and the red vinyl banquettes. The waitress approached, wearing a frilly pink dress in fuchsia and bright pink. The three of them ordered margaritas, and when she asked about food, Billy and Flattop ordered by number from the menu, and Mason ordered veggie fajitas and rice.

"Are the beans made with lard?" he said.

She smiled. "Yes, sir."

"Then hold the beans."

When she'd stepped away, Flattop leaned back and stretched his arms along the back of the booth. "So what are you doing out at Giant Rock?"

"I have to talk to somebody."

"If it's for work," Billy said, "you mean you're going to interview somebody, or debrief him, I'm thinking."

"That's the plan."

"Smack him around," Flattop said, "and put the screws to him?"

Mason laughed. "I don't do that."

"Is it one of the airstrip workers?" Billy said.

"There's not much in the way of facilities there," Flattop said. "I asked around. Apparently it's just a guy and his wife and a wind sock."

"They host a flying-saucer meet-up a few times a year," Mason said. "It's happening this weekend. I need to talk to one of the people who's going out for that."

"Flying saucers?" Flattop's eyebrows shot up. "Do you think those things are real?"

"I have no idea. What do you think?"

"So much has been written about them. There has to be something to it." He eyed Billy.

"Why not?" Billy said. "They might even be ours. I spent enough time in the military to know they're never going to tell us the whole story about anything."

The margaritas arrived, and they clinked glasses. The conversation shifted, and Mason listened to them talk about their lives, about the guys in their social circle at the Blue Moon. Gay life was a lot more marginal here, and they talked about friends who had been harassed, and arrested, and lost their jobs.

The heady drink and the meal made him tired, and riding back to their house in the high-revving little pickup, Mason felt like he could sleep right there. Before he went upstairs, he said good night, and once he was in bed he quickly sank into the dream world.

Twelve

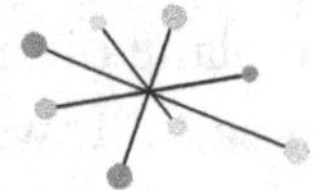

"TIME TO HIT THE road," a voice said, and Mason struggled to wake up. It was completely dark out. He blinked and eyed Billy.

"Are you OK?" Billy said.

"Where are we?" he mumbled.

"It'll come to you, Stretch."

Struggling for consciousness, he sat up and tossed the covers aside.

"Whoa—somebody sleeps in the buff."

Mason pulled the sheets over his crotch. "Sorry about that."

"I don't mind the view," he said, and chuckled, then stepped out.

Once he'd washed up, and put on his suit, Mason went downstairs.

"Do you want me to boil you an egg or something?" Billy was at the kitchen table, dressed for work in gray bib coveralls, a coffee mug in front of him.

"I'll just have some fruit." Mason pulled open the heavy fridge door and grabbed an orange. "Where's your boyfriend?"

"He wanted to get flying."

"He's taking the plane out now?"

"At sunup," Billy said. "It would have cost you the same no matter when he got started."

"Good for him. I'm glad I could help him get in the air." He poured himself a coffee from the percolator on the stove.

Billy rose and put his mug in the sink, then went into the living room. Mason heard the front door close as he sat at the table and peeled the orange, munching on the segments. He'd finished it by the time Billy got back. He'd donned a white painter's cap.

"I put your groceries in the pickup."

"Thanks, man."

"You're welcome, 'man.'" Billy chuckled. "Are you ready to go?"

Mason slurped at his mug as he got up to put it in the sink, then followed him out to the driveway. The orange glow of the eastern sky came into view as Billy backed into the street.

"You never said who you were riding with today," Billy said.

"A journalist who's going out to write about the saucer-heads."

"It's a long trip. Is he handsome, at least?"

"It's a woman."

"Hoo, boy. Do not let her do the driving."

Mason eyed him. "Why not?"

"You know what they say about woman drivers."

"I'm sure she'll do better than I would."

"I remember," Billy said. "You don't know how to double-shift, or use a choke."

"So we'll all be safer if she drives."

In front of Geraldine's building, Mason pointed out the sedan, curvy and dark in the twilight.

"That's her car."

Billy pulled up behind it and hopped out, quickly unloading the cases of water and the grocery bag from the truck bed. He set them on the grassy verge next to Geraldine's trunk.

"You're right on time," Geraldine said, walking out of the apartment's courtyard, a bulky handbag slung over one shoulder. She was wearing sneakers, and a light skirt hemmed at midcalf, and a white blouse with red polka dots on it.

"This is my friend Billy," Mason said.

"Ma'am," Billy said, and lifted his cap. "See you later," he said to Mason, and turned to walk back to his pickup.

"What's all this?" Geraldine said, eyeing the boxes and the grocery bag.

"Water and snacks. It's a long drive."

"Do you really think we'll need all that?"

"It gets hot in the Mojave in July."

She opened the trunk, and Mason lifted the boxes in and set the grocery bag beside them. As he stepped back onto the sidewalk, he saw another woman walking out of the building with a boxy red plaid suitcase in hand. Around Geraldine's age, she wore her long hair tied back, and a billowy blouse, and jeans. As she approached, she frowned and gave Mason a pointed once-over.

"This is Julia," Geraldine said. "My roommate."

"Ma'am," Mason said, and lifted his hat the way Billy had.

Ignoring him, she set the suitcase in the trunk and closed the lid.

"I saw this one yesterday," Julia said. "He was snooping around our apartment."

"Not your apartment, specifically," Mason said, feeling his face heating up. "Mr. Parker was showing me around the building."

"Are you married, Mr. Mason?" Julia said. "I don't see a ring on that finger."

"It's just Mason," he said. "And yes, I am."

"Geraldine knows jiu-jitsu, you know."

"That's great news," Mason said. "If we run into any road bandits, she can give them the chop while I run away."

Geraldine laughed, then stepped close to Julia. "I'll be fine. I'll be home before you get back from your mother's."

"Keep an eye on this guy," Julia said, eyeing Mason sidelong. "He looks handsy."

Touching her arm, Geraldine guided her up the front walk to have a private word. Mason watched from beside the car as they spoke for a moment, leaning close together. Finally Geraldine gave her a parting hug. There was definitely more than just friendship between them. That might explain why Julia was so hostile—in her eyes Mason could be a rival.

Eventually Geraldine came back, and walked around to the driver's side. Mason waited until she was behind the wheel before he climbed in. There wasn't enough headroom for his hat, so he pulled it off and tossed it in the back. There were no seatbelts on the big bench seat, he realized, scrabbling for them and finding none. That made for a worrisome start.

Geraldine started the engine and pulled away from the curb. The car rode smooth compared to Billy's pickup, and she seemed like a confident driver, easily maneuvering the big vehicle.

The sun was coming up, but it was still early, and the streets weren't busy. Geraldine seemed a little on edge, Mason thought, eyeing her. Yesterday she'd been suspicious of him, but this felt different. From her perspective, maybe he could understand—he was a total stranger, and a big mooky guy, and her roommate had just warned her that he would likely try to assault her.

"I had the oil changed this week, in preparation for the trip," Geraldine said. "I had the mechanic look over the engine too. He said we shouldn't have any trouble."

"That's great news."

"I also checked the map. The place where I turn off the main road is just before Twentynine Palms. You'll only have to find your own way for the last few miles."

"I'm sure there'll be enough traffic to get a ride."

Geraldine navigated toward the 101, and merged into the southbound traffic. The freeway wasn't finished yet, he saw, with a big construction site at Bunker Hill. As she picked up speed she seemed to be steering a lot, as if the car wasn't that stable, and she gripped the top of the wheel with both hands.

"You never asked me why I'm going out to the Mojave," Geraldine said.

That was a stupid oversight on his part—he

already knew, but of course she didn't know that.

"There's something I've been meaning to ask you, Geraldine," he said. "Why are you going out to the Mojave today?"

She laughed. "Well, there's a flying-saucer convention. I'm going to write about it."

"You're a journalist?"

"And a fiction writer."

"How fun is that?"

"I'm so glad you didn't laugh at me."

"Why would I laugh at your work?" Mason said. "It's not my place to judge you, or the flying-saucer group."

"Most people have their minds made up in advance. They're either certain that it's bunkum, or they're excited about the topic." She eyed him sidelong. "Do you believe in flying saucers?"

"I have no reason to disbelieve them. I've never seen one up close, but I have seen some strange things in the night sky."

"Like what?" she demanded, glancing at him again.

Mason told her about the colored orbs he'd seen, and the lights that Ned said looked like RV headlights.

"Where did you see all this?"

"Kind of where we're headed. In the Mojave, near Twentynine Palms."

"There's something big happening, don't you

think? It's time for a sea change." She sat up and leaned toward the steering wheel. "Hang on. I need to pay attention to the road for a minute."

Geraldine guided the big car to the right and exited the freeway, looping under it and onto a wide boulevard. Mason pulled the visor down to block the low sun. He had no idea where they were, but it was well south of downtown. They passed a road sign that implied they were on U.S. 99, and then on the left a street sign said this was Garvey Boulevard. He'd never heard of either one.

Once they were at cruising speed again, Geraldine spoke.

"I'm so glad I ran into you. An open-minded person is much better company than a skeptic."

"I know enough about the world to know it's not simple. There's a lot more to it than what the physical senses perceive."

"You sound like a mystic."

"I'm not," Mason said. "But I'm also not a skeptic."

"You won't get any pushback from me. I'm metaphysically inclined myself."

"Have you heard of the idea that there are no coincidences?"

"So you think it was meant to be, us riding together?" Geraldine said. A smile played on her lips.

"Maybe. What evidence have you seen that

makes you think the flying saucers are real?"

"They're here—they've landed," she said, and told him about several saucer sightings she'd read about, and encounters with their occupants. One of the stories was familiar from some of the reading he'd done, but others he'd never heard before. There were a lot of encounters, and Geraldine remembered a lot of detail, even the way the witnesses had described the craft.

As he listened he watched the scenery roll by, built-up areas interspersed with green space, and even some orchards. Off to the left the ridgeline of the hills looked familiar. Those had to be the ones around Whittier. Recognizing that, plus the fact that the sun was in their eyes, meant they were indeed headed east.

"I feel like I'm talking a lot," Geraldine said finally.

"Fine by me. It's interesting stuff."

"In any case, considering everything I've read, I'm certain that the space brothers are coming from other planets in our system, not from other stars."

"Why is that?"

"It's too far. The next star is many light years away. No one knows whether other stars even have planets. Mars and Venus are so close. It makes more sense that they're coming from relatively nearby."

"How about this idea," Mason said. "The space brothers aren't from another physical place. They're from another version of reality. It's right here, all around us. You just can't sense it."

She eyed him for a moment. "Now, that would make for great science fiction."

They were in another town, and Geraldine braked for a red light. It was hard to believe she could even see them—they were tiny, just dim little red dots at the side of the road. He was glad she was driving and not him. Past the stoplight she slowed down again and pulled into a gas station. A guy in pin-striped coveralls came out of the garage and stepped up to the pump. Geraldine rolled down the window to talk to him.

"Fill it, please."

"Want me to check under the hood?"

"It's fine," she said.

Mason climbed out and stretched. The sun was getting higher, and it was always warmer inland. He pulled off his suit jacket and threw it in the backseat with his fedora, amid the array of magazines, and books, and a straw hat.

When the attendant hung the nozzle back on the pump, Mason stepped around to speak to him.

"What's the damage?"

"Five eight-two," he said, wiping his hands.

Mason dug a fin and a single out of his pocket

and handed it over. "Keep the change."

"Thanks, mac." He stuffed the bills into his pocket and walked back toward the garage.

"You tipped him?" Geraldine demanded as he got into the car.

"Is that not customary?"

"Not around here, Mr. Moneybags."

"It was just a few cents."

She started the engine and pulled back onto the boulevard, gradually accelerating to highway speed.

"I brought a newsletter about the flying-saucer meeting," she said, "if you're interested. In the back."

Mason leaned over the seat and dug around. Under his jacket was a clipboard, and a legal pad, and a sheaf of what looked like notes in blue ballpoint. Among them he found a typewritten newsletter. He'd actually seen this already, he realized, sitting down again and leafing through it. It had been scanned into the Giant Rock guy's FBI file.

"It says the meet-up is in March, not July," Mason said.

"I have another issue at home that talks about the event this weekend. Don't worry—I'm sure I have the right dates."

"This says bring your own food and camping equipment."

"It is a little rough out there. I was planning to sleep in the car."

Mason tossed the newsletter in the backseat. "So tell me about the fiction you've written."

"I work in the science fiction genre. Right now I'm trying to sell some short stories to magazines. One is about explorers on Mars who unexpectedly meet aliens. Another is space prospectors who discover the asteroids were once a planet that was destroyed in a hydrogen-bomb battle."

"I'd totally read those."

"I'm hawking them under a male pseudonym—Jerry. Lots of people don't think women can write science fiction."

"Bullshit," Mason said. "Gender makes no difference."

She eyed him. "You sound like an enlightened man."

"Social norms like that just seem like bullshit to me. I'm sure other people can see it too."

"Coarse," Geraldine said, "but enlightened."

"Excuse my language."

She waved a hand. "I'm not a prude. But I can't agree that all social norms are useless."

"How about what you just said, then? It assumes that women can't think as clearly as men. It's an old idea, but we both know it's not true. What if Emily Dickinson had believed she shouldn't write, or Gertrude Stein?"

"I'm no Emily Dickinson," Geraldine said. "Maybe we have to do what's right for us individually. That's my approach. I chose to work independently, rather than sitting at a typewriter and making coffee for some fresh banker."

"I get it. I've always been happier not being in an office."

They rode in silence for a while, as the boulevard started to look more like a highway, drifting in and out of towns less frequently.

"So what about our personal choices," Mason said. "Do you think what we do is mostly predetermined? Or is it up to chance and our own decisions? If someone told you a calamity was heading your way, would you be able to avoid it?"

"Such a serious question. Cleanthes thought we didn't have much choice, like the story about the dog and the cart."

"Who's she? I don't know that story."

"He's a he." Geraldine laughed. "One of the Stoics. It's a metaphor for the human experience. He said a dog leashed to a cart can't just go wherever it wants, so it's easiest if it just follows the cart. Resisting the cart's momentum only leads to pain."

"So our lives are predetermined, just like the dog's path is inevitable."

"There's some choice, the thinking goes, but not much."

"Is life really like that?"

"The Stoics thought it was."

"What do you think?" Mason said, watching her.

"Maybe we have less choice than we assume we do. To me it feels like I have unlimited options. The world is there for the taking. And if I knew there was a calamity ahead, I hope I'd be able to avoid it." She waved a hand. "There's probably more to the cart metaphor. I remember it from college, but I'm no philosopher."

"I think a lot of what happens to us is just random chance. Good luck and bad luck. Maybe with the right kind of nudge, you can make good choices and avoid the worst of it."

"Avoid the calamities."

Mason looked out at the highway. "Let's hope so."

Thirteen

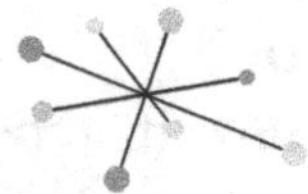

THEY DROVE THROUGH A few miles of road construction, slowing to a crawl where the pavement ended and the dirt had been rolled flat. Instead of traffic cones to demarcate the lanes there were oil torches—little black spheres with an orange flame burning at the top. They looked exactly like the oversize hand grenades the characters would throw at each other in old cartoons.

Past the construction zone the highway widened to the point that it felt like a freeway. The sky was blue and cloudless, like it usually was, and Mason looked up when a glint of sunlight caught his eye. It was an airplane, khaki green, with propellers on each wing, flying low over the road and sinking toward the earth ahead of them.

"There must be an airport over there," Mason said, watching it descend.

"It might be Morrow Field."

Mason had never heard of it, but other aircraft tails were visible now, lined up in series, near where the plane had disappeared.

"Oh, no," Geraldine said, raising her voice.

"What's going on?"

Then Mason saw it too—wisps of steam escaping from the front end of the car. She pulled to the left and turned across the oncoming lanes, onto a side road, then stopped on the gravel and killed the engine.

"Is it the radiator?" Mason said.

"Of course it's the radiator."

With the engine off, he could hear its angry hiss.

"So what do we do?"

She turned to look at him. "Has this never happened to you before?"

"I guess not."

Geraldine took a deep breath. "We wait for the motor to cool off, then we drive to a service station to refill the radiator with antifreeze."

"Should we take off the cap? It would cool down more quickly."

"Let me answer that question with another question," she said. "Do you want to get scalded?"

"OK," he said. "I get it. How about a drink?"

Normally on a relentlessly sunny day like this he would have slathered on a ton of sunscreen, but the fedora served the same purpose. He grabbed it from the backseat and pulled it on as he climbed out and walked back to the trunk. Geraldine got out and unlocked it for him, then went to lift the hood. The billowing steam had subsided, but he could still hear it hissing. He stepped around and handed her a bottle of water, then opened his own, and they stood beside the car to drink.

"I didn't wear my watch," she said. "I wonder what time it is?"

"I don't have my phone," Mason said, and took another swig.

Geraldine shot him a puzzled look. "I made a couple of chicken salad sandwiches. Would you like one?"

"I can't eat chicken. Thanks anyway. I'll have an apple."

She went to the trunk for her sandwich, wrapped in wax paper, and tossed one of the apples underhand to Mason. He managed to catch it against his shirt, inelegantly, and they ate leaning on the rear fender. The only sounds were him biting into the crisp fruit and the passing vehicles on the nearby highway.

"Do you have a trash bag?" Mason said, straightening up.

"I don't. You need it for your apple core?"

"I'm not sure what to do with it. I guess I could leave it in the trunk."

Geraldine frowned and waggled her fingers for it. When he handed it over, she wound up and hurled it overhand into the weedy ditch that ran beside the road, then looked at him, her eyebrows arching above her sunglasses.

"That works too," he said. "Listen, that airport is right up this road—do you think they'd have antifreeze?"

"I don't know if airplanes use it, but they might have some for their cars. We won't be able to drive over there for a while yet."

"I'll walk over and ask." He straightened his tie and tucked his shirt in. "Do you think I need to wear my suit jacket?"

She suppressed a smile. "I don't think it matters."

Mason set off, walking up the road, assuming his rapid commuter pace. There was a sign that said MORROW FIELD at the driveway, but there was no gate, and as he approached the hangar, he saw that several small planes were parked next to it. There was a fuel pump out front, but no security at all. This was before the skyjacking epidemic and all the terrorist attacks—anyone could come in and drive onto the runway if they wanted.

He tried the door beside the fuel pumps, and it opened, ringing a little bell overhead as he stepped in. It was a spartan front office that connected to the cavernous hangar space behind it, where a small airplane was parked, its tail illuminated by the daylight from the big open doors.

A guy with wild wavy red hair stepped in from the hangar, wiping his hands on a rag.

"Can I help you?" he said.

"I need to buy some coolant for a car. Would you have any of that?"

His eyes narrowed. "You mean antifreeze?"

"That's the stuff."

"I can sell you some, sure. Just one can?"

"How much does a car typically need?" Mason said.

"It comes in quart cans. I doubt you'd need more than one of those."

"Maybe I'll take two. It might boil over again."

"Give me a minute," he said, and went back into the hangar. When he reappeared, he had two squat cans in hand.

"What are they worth?" Mason said, digging in his pants pocket.

"A buck even."

Mason set two singles on the counter. The guy picked them up, then hesitated, and handed one back.

"I meant a buck for both," he said.

"Got it." Mason pocketed the dollar and picked up the cans. "Thanks for being an honest man."

"I'm not going to stiff a fellow redhead. I know you get enough grief."

Walking back to the road, he saw that each can had a little metal handle on the top, so he carried them that way, one dangling from each arm.

When Geraldine spotted him walking back toward the car, she broke into a smile.

"You found some."

He set the cans on the ground. "Do you think the radiator will be cool enough by now?"

"It's not steaming anymore. Use your handkerchief to open it, just in case."

Mason frowned. "So I'm the one who's doing it? It's your car."

Geraldine put her hands on her hips. "You said you were good with repairs."

"Fine. But I don't actually have a hankie."

"There might be a cloth in the trunk," she said, and stepped around to the back, returning a moment later with a gray cotton rag.

Mason folded it up and held it at arm's length to turn the radiator cap. It hissed angrily when it popped open, but it didn't explode. He snatched his hand away as it came loose, just in case, then gingerly felt the cap. It wasn't too hot to touch.

"Should the tank be completely full?" he said, twisting the cap off one of the cans of coolant.

"I assume so." She frowned. "I can't believe you don't have any experience with this."

"I don't have a car," he said, and poured the red liquid into the radiator. It took most of the quart before the level was at the top.

He wanted to ask her to check whether he'd put the radiator cap on correctly, but he resisted the impulse, and carried the cans of coolant to the trunk. Once Geraldine had slammed the hood down, she got in and started the engine.

"Purring like a kitten," she said, and popped it into gear, then pulled a U-turn.

"Are you sure this car can get us there?" Mason said. "The high desert is quite a climb. Three thousand feet up from the Coachella Valley."

"This is a Packard," she said, craning over the wheel to check for traffic. "It'll be fine."

As if to demonstrate, she punched the accelerator and roared across the westbound lanes, veering left onto the highway. Soon they were at cruising speed, and followed the road up through the hills. With less development around, it was starting to look like the route he knew, where the 10 climbed toward the Gorgonio Pass.

Mason opened the vent panel in the side window to let some air in. It was getting hotter, and drier.

"I have to say, I admire your independence," he said. "You have your own job, and your own car."

"Oh, you are a honey dripper." She briefly pulled her sunglasses down to shoot him a look. "You can ask me out anytime."

"That's never going to happen, sister."

"I remember you told Julia you were married. Is that why?"

"I guess I am, sort of."

She laughed. "Sort of?"

"You know how it is," Mason said, and looked out his window. "Besides, you already have options."

"How would you know?"

"I met Julia."

"She's a girl, in case you hadn't noticed."

"A girl who cares about you—a lot," Mason said. "She basically read me the riot act this morning."

Geraldine didn't reply to that, and when Mason glanced at her, he saw that she was blushing. It was telling that she didn't refute it.

"Julia is just a good friend," she said finally.

"I'd bet money she'd be up for more than that, if you were," he said. "She'd be a better match for you than that woman you left your cat with."

She glared at him. "How do you know who I left my cat with?"

Mason sat up. He'd let himself get too comfortable. Why had he said that?

"Well, I think you mentioned you left your cat with someone," he said, trying to think quickly.

"I don't remember saying anything about it." Her voice rose. "Mason, what's going on?"

"We were talking before about your metaphysical inclinations," he said. "There's something I didn't tell you."

She threw up a hand, a tacit demand for him to explain.

"I'm kind of psychic."

"In what way?"

"I can see things sometimes."

"Like my cat? And my friend Margaret?"

"Not in so much detail. I can prove it to you, if you want."

Geraldine scoffed. "I very much doubt that."

"I can read things. Metal objects, like keys and jewelry. Let me try."

She didn't reply to that, but a moment later she moved her hands together at the top of the steering wheel and pulled a ring off her right hand.

"What does that tell you?" she said, holding it out to him. It was a silver band with a small pink stone.

"Put it on the seat. I have to prepare my mind first."

"Oh, of course," she said, setting it down. "There's a procedure."

"You believe in the space brothers, but you're skeptical about psychic power? That's messed up."

She waved a hand. "Let's just see what you can do."

Mason huffed and closed his eyes, working to clear his mind. It took a while to sweep away the random noise. The constant hum of the tires on the pavement gave him a point of focus, and once his mind was blank he picked up the ring, and held it in his left hand, and covered it with his right.

The metal felt cool. Nothing came to him at first, but then he got an image. It was outside somewhere, a landscape, flat and monotone. Winter, he realized—there was snow in the air, blown by the wind in billowing sheets. He could almost hear the sound of it. It was dark here—nighttime.

"You were somewhere flat," Mason said, opening his eyes. "The wind was blowing, and there was snow, but it was dark. Like black snow."

Geraldine gestured for the ring and took it back, slipping it onto her finger.

"Not bad," she said finally. "This belonged to my Great Aunt Bess. She came to California during the dust bowl on the Great Plains. One of her stories was about the blowing dirt. There was so much of it in the air that it felt like nighttime.

The dirt would get into everything, she said. Every crack and corner."

"So there you go. Psychic power."

"I'm still not sure how you got a psychic vision of the friend who's taking care of my cat."

"Not really a vision. Just a general impression."

She eyed him sidelong. "I'm sorry, Mason. It's just so tenuous."

"So are the space brothers," he said, and folded his arms.

They rode in silence for a while. Mason gazed out the window, watching the hilly landscape, and saw a road sign for Yucaipa. He knew where that was. He wished he could get a coffee—right now he was feeling completely wiped out.

"You don't talk about yourself much," Geraldine said. "Not like most men. Where are you from?"

"Los Angeles," he said absently, not looking at her.

"But you're just moving there, you said. Where were you before that?"

He needed to focus, he realized. That was the thing about lying—it took a lot more concentration to remember all the details.

"Have you heard of Pittsfield, Massachusetts?"

"That's a General Electric town."

"That's the one," he said, even though he wasn't sure what she meant.

"What took you to D.C.? Were you a G-man?"

He'd shown her his driver's license, he remembered. "You mean Washington. I lived there for a couple of years, but I never worked for Uncle Sam."

"The D.C. connection makes me wonder if you're an FBI agent sent to spy on the saucer meetings. Is that how you knew about Margaret?"

"I'm not spying on anyone, and I don't work for the feds."

"If you were undercover," she said, "you'd have to say that. You couldn't tell me about it."

"So I guess you'll never know for sure either way. One piece of evidence you should consider, though—a G-man would probably be able to get a vehicle to use from the motor pool. I wouldn't be hitching a ride."

Geraldine sighed. "As a fiction writer, I can say that your flimflam would make a good starting point for a short story."

Mason frowned, and felt his face reddening. "It's not flimflam."

"I'm not saying you're a spy," Geraldine said, with a languorous gesture. "Not necessarily. But I know you're not telling me the whole truth. I'm sure you have your reasons. Like you said, I'm in no position to judge. Lots of people want to forget the last decade. The horror of it. But it's a new era. Things are changing fast. You can understand why I want to focus on looking ahead."

"Looking ahead, and looking up," Mason said. "There's saucers out there. Keep your eyes on the skies."

She laughed. "That's a very good idea."

Fourteen

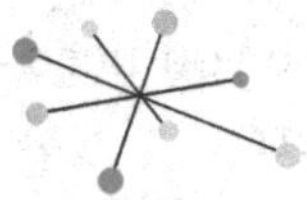

THE CAR MADE IT into the Coachella Valley without incident. It was so much warmer here, and drier than it had been in April. They cracked the windows to compensate for the lack of air-conditioning. Mason reached into the backseat for his bottle of water, and offered Geraldine the one she'd been drinking from.

"That's the highway to Palm Springs," she said, slowing the car. "Do we go that way?"

"The road to the high desert is on the left," Mason said, "and it's not for a few more miles."

She nodded and kept going, and when they came to the turn, signposted for Twentynine

Palms, she made the left.

"It's not far now," she said. "There's a little settlement when we get to the top. I can drop you there."

"I was thinking about that. Maybe I can go to Twentynine Palms later on. I'd like to see what's happening at the saucer event."

Geraldine smiled. "I've piqued your interest."

"How could I miss out on this? I'm metaphysically inclined, just like you are."

"It's not because you need to prepare a report for J. Edgar Hoover?"

"I don't know her," Mason said. "Is she one of the space brothers?"

"J. Edgar is a he." She glanced over at him. "I never know when to take you seriously."

"That suits me."

The pavement ended after the first big hill, and the climb on the unsurfaced road went slow. The car managed to crest the final rise without overheating again. There was less settlement here, but the land didn't look that different from what he'd seen a few weeks ago—he knew exactly where he was, and they were headed straight east again. When they passed the turn for Pioneertown, Mason pointed it out.

"Less than two miles from here to the turnoff," he said.

"How do you know?"

"Just watch the odometer."

He could feel his heart pounding—this was the critical moment, the choice that mattered. A sign appeared, marked THE WINDMILLS, with an arrow pointing left.

"That's the turn," he said, sitting up and jabbing his finger at the windshield.

"I don't think it is," she said, not slowing down. "It's a little farther."

As they passed the corner, Mason shouted, "Stop! Stop the car."

Geraldine hit the brakes and veered over to the shoulder, then turned to scowl at him. "Don't shout at me. That's not the right way."

"I'm telling you it is. You have to turn there, or we'll get lost."

"Calm down. I've been here before. I'm certain the road is farther east."

Mason took a breath. He probably should have had a better plan to deal with this dispute.

"When you were out here before, were you driving?" he said.

"No—but neither were you. You're being awfully bossy for someone who's never been to Giant Rock."

"Earlier today you talked about being independent. Doing things for yourself. But sometimes you have to let other people help you."

"You're not helping me," she said. "You're

misleading me."

"What do you want to do with your life?" Mason demanded. "You're kind of at a crossroads here. You either go to the saucer meet-up, or you head for a dead-end road in the sand."

She watched him for a moment. "You know what I want to do. I told you. I'm going to meet the saucer people, and I'm going to write about them."

"Consider this—if I'm wrong about this road, it's still completely safe to be too far west. Think about the lay of the land. There are mesas and mountains and all of Big Bear flanking the west side of the basin. If we're too far west, we'll be forced to go east. But if you're wrong, and we go too far east, there's just a whole lot of empty desert, from here to the Colorado River." He waved an arm. "Remember the thing about the impending calamity? You need to choose wisely. Choose to avoid it. Going farther east is the calamity."

Geraldine slowly shook her head. "Men," she said flatly. "I thought you were different."

She put the car in gear, and to Mason's great relief, made a U-turn, and then slowed down to make the turn. This was the right way. He'd done it—in this moment, for a while at least, he'd changed her destiny.

After they'd gone a few miles, Geraldine

spoke. "This doesn't look like the road I was on before."

"That saucer meet-up newsletter says the turnoff is marked with a sign. It's about fifteen miles."

The road got narrower, and rougher, with washboards in places. It sank rapidly into a big wash and then up again onto the higher ground, studded with Joshua trees. Mason was surprised the car could handle the steep incline without trouble. The scattered homestead cabins and ranch fences gradually became sparser.

"By the odometer we've come fifteen miles," Geraldine said. "This road is starting to angle west. We're going to wind up in Victorville— that's halfway home again."

"Just keep going," Mason said. "I'm sure it's only another mile or so."

"I'm really not sure about this."

"I'm sure," he said.

Before she could protest again, a sign came into view, on the side of the road: GIANT ROCK AIRPORT.

"You were right," Geraldine said. "I can hardly believe it."

"What a relief, right? Landers is just a couple miles, then it's straight north to Giant Rock."

"What's Landers?" she said. "Is that in the newsletter?"

"I just mean the crossroads. I think there'll be another sign."

Even though the road narrowed until it was just a double track in the desert, Geraldine didn't question his navigation again. It was clear when they'd arrived at Giant Rock, with the dozens of cars parked around, and the oversize boulder that dominated the landscape. Flat open desert stretched to the right of it, and the rocky hillside behind. Most striking since he'd last seen it was that the rock was still an intact mass—the chunk on this side of it hadn't cleaved off yet.

In the hills he could see a canvas wind shelter held up by ropes, along with the tops of some tents nestled among the rocks. A couple of camping trailers were parked with the vehicles, and beyond the cars three airplane tails were visible, lined up in a neat row. Right in front of the rock itself was a wooden platform, maybe fifteen feet high, painted white and with stairs leading up behind it. No one was up there now, but lots of people were sitting around in the sunshine, eating and talking.

Geraldine pulled up beside a station wagon and killed the engine, then pulled the rearview mirror toward her and adjusted her hair.

"I did it," she said.

"You did indeed."

Mason had to smile. He wanted to give her a

high-five, but it wouldn't mean anything to her. She reached into the backseat for her straw hat and her notebook.

"It looks so bohemian, doesn't it? We should go talk to people."

"You don't need me to get in your way. We'll split up."

They climbed out, and Mason pulled his hat low over his eyes for the bright sun. Even though it was too hot to wear it, he took his suit jacket and draped it over his shoulder.

"Can you open the trunk before you go?" he said. "I want more water."

Geraldine took a bottle for herself, and tucked it under her arm, and strode toward the crowd. After he'd drunk deeply, Mason took an apple, and pocketed another to eat later. There was still a case and a half of water in here for Geraldine's return trip, just in case she got lost.

He slammed the trunk lid, then walked toward the rock, munching on his apple. The hills behind it rose gradually to similar heights, but here at the edge, the rock towered over the desert flats. Devoid of graffiti, it felt grander now, and more dramatic, worthier of its name.

As he got closer, up in the rocks he saw a family having lunch at a card table they'd set up next to one of the tents, two women and a man and some children. A pair of umbrellas resting open on a rock acted as their sun shade.

Skirting the edge of the crowd of people, who sat on folding chairs and long benches in front of the wooden platform, he realized he was getting inquisitive looks from some of them. It had to be what he was wearing, the suit and tie, when everyone else was dressed for camping. Guys were in casual shirtsleeves, and denim, and chinos. Like Geraldine, lots of the women wore straw hats, and skirts, and pants. There were cowboy hats and even a pith helmet or two. Everyone here was white and Anglo, he realized, but they were all ages, and Geraldine was right—it felt bohemian.

It must be a lunch break, he decided. The platform was where the speakers would be when things got going. He spotted Geraldine over near the base of it, talking to a man and a woman, all of them looking earnest in their discussion.

Around behind the rock he found a little food counter, built right under the stone, and a doorway next to it. Matt had pointed this out as the room underneath the rock, where the host lived, but it was padlocked now.

When he walked back toward the crowd, he saw a guy in a suit climbing the platform. This was the only other person he'd seen here who was wearing a necktie. It wasn't the airstrip proprietor, he knew, as he'd seen that guy's photo. This had to be one of the guest speakers.

People started to move closer to the platform, filling the benches just below. Geraldine sat cross-legged on the sand, gazing up at the speaker, her notepad in hand. The guy wasn't amplified, but people got quiet to listen to him, and from his perch he was loud enough to be heard.

"Greetings, brothers and sisters," he began, and went on to talk about how he was receiving psychic messages from the occupants of the saucers. His talk followed the familiar theme: the space brothers were concerned about the welfare of the human species, and specifically the risks of atomic weapons. At one point he pulled out a sheaf of paper and read a message from them, telepathically dictated for this very event:

> Many of your fellow beings will suffer illness from your atomic experiments. Using atomic power for destruction will rebound on the users. The forces of destruction must be put aside for a greater awakening. Human consciousness must yield to the age of peace and light.

It sounded kind of vague, and the tone was definitely something that would make a xeno-phobe suspicious, but the crowd was rapt, com-pletely tuned in and focused on him. Mason didn't need to listen to it, he decided. He'd read enough of this stuff.

Walking back toward the parked cars, it

looked like there were definitely more of them parked here now. A woman was setting up a photo exhibit, using clothespins to clip eight-by-ten black-and-white prints to a cord strung between two vehicles. The photos were of old-timey saucers, like what he'd seen in the early contactee material.

Next to her, a guy had a table set up in front of a jeep, with an array of T-shirts for sale. As he walked by, the guy met his eye.

"You're all dressed up," he said. "You should ditch the necktie and put on a T-shirt."

"I know I'm totally overdressed," Mason said. Stepping closer, he saw that the shirts bore a silk-screened drawing of a saucer zooming out of a cloud. The guy was wearing one of them. He gestured to the parked cars. "Is this typical of the crowd size at these events?"

"There'll be more people here tomorrow and Sunday," he said.

"Are there speakers all three days?"

"That's right." He folded his arms. "Most people who come out here already know the score. You have a lot of questions. And the suit—it makes me wonder if you're undercover."

"If I were undercover, I'd be dressed like you." Mason raised his eyebrows. "I'm not a G-man, if that's what you're thinking. I'm in insurance. I just came by for the day."

"Well, you should stick around for the evening. The real action happens after dark."

"Do you actually see UFOs?"

"Of course." He frowned. "We all do. The rock is an earth energy vortex. Just being here attracts the saucers."

Mason nodded. "That would make sense."

"So are you going to buy a shirt?"

"I can't," he said. "But don't leave this stuff out overnight. The space brothers in the long pink spacecraft tend to steal."

His eyes grew wide. "Why would they do that?"

"They're not malicious. It's just their culture. If something isn't in your hand, to them it means nobody owns it, so it's not wrong to take it."

"That's so interesting. They sound like communists. What's their species called?"

"I don't know. But their heads are longer than ours, and they have hair like pinfeathers. Their complexion is really red."

"Redder than yours?"

"You're funny," Mason said, and frowned. "My complexion wasn't designed for the desert sun."

"Well, I'll keep my eye peeled."

A woman stepped up to look at the shirts, and Mason moved away. Walking past the cars, he went over to the airplanes, parked at the edge of the dirt runway. At one side of it a small boulder had been painted white and had a wind sock attached to the top. He hadn't seen Flattop around—these planes belonged to the fly-in saucer-heads.

The runway stretched into the flat landscape, dipping slightly at a white salt pan. Mason walked toward it, squinting in the bright daylight, and shifted his hat lower over his brow. This was such a stark and beautiful place.

Movement over the distant rocky hills caught his attention. It was an airplane, he realized, and it gradually grew larger, sinking closer to the earth. It was definitely going to land here. He walked over to the side of the runway to watch it touch down.

The wheels hit the ground with a puff of dust, and the aircraft slowed as it got closer. It was white, with red stripes, and the wings were mounted over the cabin. The engine sounded like the loudest lawnmower he'd ever heard. As it taxied past, he saw a blond head in the cockpit—Flattop.

It rolled up next to the other aircraft and stopped. As Mason walked over, the engine died, and Flattop climbed out. He was wearing jeans and a leather jacket, and smiled when he recognized Mason, then paused to peel off the jacket and throw it back into the plane.

"It's warm out here," he said, as Mason approached. "I can't believe all these people came so far for a flying-saucer convention."

"It's a great place for it, don't you think? The rock is so dramatic."

"Listen, I need to drain the snake, and maybe get some coffee."

"I'm in no rush," Mason said. "Have a look around. Just come and find me whenever you're ready to go."

Flattop clapped him on the shoulder, and they walked toward the rock. No one was on the platform now, and Mason stood among the benches as Flattop walked around to where the concession was. Geraldine was standing with a cluster of people, over at the base of the platform, intent in their conversation. The guy who was talking was waving his arms. He couldn't hear the words, but his body language demonstrated his intensity. Mason had to grin. That's why Geraldine had come out here—to hear all this stuff firsthand.

The nudge he'd given her, the change in her path—it really had changed her outcome. Maybe it had taken more than just that moment on the road, and the nudge had been about the entire morning, the lengthy trip from the city. In some way the shift had to have happened with her subconscious assent—him changing things really meant Geraldine letting him change her mind.

Hopefully it would stick. If Peggy was right, reality would just adjust slightly to achieve the same outcome, and Geraldine might not even survive the day. But then why would Hanh have let him do this, go to all this trouble, if that were going to happen? Maybe it was a lesson in humility, he realized—to demonstrate to him the futility of coming here, the pointlessness of meddling, his inability to truly change things. That was a dark thought.

As if sensing his gaze, Geraldine looked toward him. He nodded, and she smiled, then went back to her conversation. When Flattop appeared, he had a hamburger in one hand and a paper cup in the other.

"These saucer nuts have good food," he said. "You should get one."

"The snack bar was closed when I went by. Do they have coffee?"

"Unfortunately not. This is just water."

"I'm good with my apple," Mason said, and dug it out of his pocket.

"Once I'm done with this, we can leave whenever you're ready."

"Let me say good-bye to my contact," Mason said.

When he approached Geraldine, she stepped away from the group and flashed him a smile, her eyes bright. He knew how she felt, knew the head space she was in, that exhilarating experience of getting a bunch of new ideas all at once. She really was in her element here.

"I've got a ride," he said, "so I'm leaving."

Geraldine reached for his hand and gave it a squeeze. "I enjoyed getting to know you today."

"Me too. Take care of yourself."

"I'm sure I'll see you in the neighborhood."

"Try to get someone to ride back with you," Mason said. "It'll be safer."

"It'll be easier not to get lost on the way home, wouldn't you say?"

Mason grinned. "I hope so."

Flattop had finished his snack, and when Mason joined him, he led the way to his airplane.

"Not a cloud in the sky," Flattop said. "There's a little headwind, but we'll still make good time."

"How long is the trip?"

"About an hour."

"That's such good news," Mason said. "It took half the day to get out here."

The little craft barely had room for two people, especially someone of Mason's stature, and he had to slouch for his head to fit. When Flattop started the engine, it turned over a few times before it caught. The roar was startlingly loud. He revved it even higher, then started rolling, and pulled a loop back onto the runway. Craning forward, he looked up at the sky. That must be the unstaffed desert airstrip version of air-traffic control, Mason realized.

Satisfied there was no one else in the immediate vicinity, Flattop revved the engine higher and started to roll toward the salt pan, gaining speed and eventually lifting off. The sensation was more like a roller coaster hitting bottom than a commercial airliner, and the sudden upward lurch gave Mason an adrenaline rush.

The engine noise made it hard to talk, so once the ground was far enough below them that it felt safe, he contented himself with watching the scenery. At this height there was a great view of Mount San Gorgonio and the other peaks around Big Bear. Flattop headed south toward Mount San Jacinto and the Coachella Valley. It was basically the same route they'd driven to get here, but in the air it went a lot faster.

Once they were out of the desert, in the valleys closer to the coastal basin, there was still a lot of open land, green space and farmland and orchards. The city had a palpable hazy pall hanging over it. Mason knew where they were when he spotted the distinctive ziggurat crowning city hall in the distance. It was still the tallest building around.

Flattop flew south of it, descending toward a lone runway, occasionally dipping the wings left or right to maintain his alignment with the looming gray strip. On the roof of an adjacent hangar, big letters spelled out VAIL.

The bumpy landing process got Mason's heart pounding again, but at least they'd made it to the ground in one piece. Flattop taxied over to a gravel apron and stopped next to some other light planes. When he killed the engine, Mason waggled his jaw to pop his ears, relieved that it was suddenly so much quieter.

As they climbed out, Mason said, "What airport is this?"

"Don't forget your hat," Flattop said. "It's called Vail Field. It's mostly for air freight. They're closing it soon so they can build over it with warehouses."

That's why he'd never heard of it, Mason realized, reaching behind the seat for his fedora and then closing the door.

"Grab that anchor for me, would you?"

Flattop pointed to a little tire lying on the gravel. Stepping over to it, Mason saw that it was filled with concrete and had a length of rope attached. He had to use both hands to lift it. Flattop was tying the rope from a similar weight to the left wingtip, then stepped around and deftly tied the one Mason had brought to the other wing.

"Now it won't blow away?" Mason said.

Flattop smiled. "That's right."

They walked around the end of the hangar to the parking lot, and Flattop stepped up to a convertible and climbed in. It was orange, and odd-looking, with a grille that looked like a jeep and a back end that looked like a sedan.

"What kind of car is this?"

"It's called a Jeepster. From the same company that made jeeps during the war."

"I can see the jeep vibe in the front end," Mason said. "It's very cool."

Flattop eyed him as he started the engine, his brow furrowing. "Thanks, daddy-o."

The car rode rough, and it was noisy without the top up, but not nearly as loud as the airplane. Once they were back at his house, he pulled into the driveway around the corner from Billy's, and led Mason inside, then through the connecting door. Billy was stretched out on the sofa, and quickly got up when they stepped in.

"Sorry—I was just having a snooze."

"It's your house," Mason said. "You don't have to apologize."

"How was Giant Rock?"

"Productive."

"You got to interview your quarry?"

"I did—and I achieved what I needed to. I'm going to be on my way."

"Tonight?" Flattop said, and frowned. "You're welcome to stay over again. You know we have the room."

"You guys are the best," Mason said. "But I need to get home. It's been a long day."

He pulled Flattop into a hug, and then Billy, eliciting a surprised laugh. Once he'd said good-bye, he went out to the street, and donned his hat, and took a deep breath. He felt completely exhausted.

The sun was low in the northwest as he walked toward Sunset, and found the alley where he'd arrived. It was past business hours, and no one was around, not even the drunk who'd been here before. He wasn't able to find the distinctively shaped pothole at first, and he worried that it might have been altered in the last few days. But when he triangulated its location, using the doorways and the position of the fenceposts, there it was.

Standing in front of it, he closed his eyes, and breathed deeply, and took a minute to focus his energy, welling it up like a ball of light in his chest. Would Hanh even be able to find him? But he pushed that fear away, and thought about her, and Ned, and home, and visualized projecting his energy to her, imagining that she was standing right in front of him.

He was breathing hard now, his eyes squeezed shut. Suddenly he felt a hand on his shoulder, yanking him backward.

Fifteen

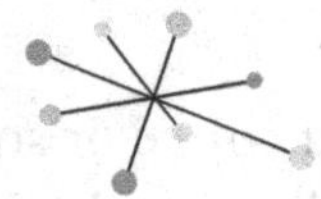

MASON STUMBLED AND TWISTED sideways, blinded in the sudden darkness,
but he managed not to tumble to the
ground. He gasped at the cold air, and blinked,
trying to get his bearings. Hanh was here, he saw,
barely visible in the dim light.

"Home again," she said, her tone light.

Struggling to focus, he managed to say, "You
found me."

"Have you achieved what you set out to do?"

"I did, but I suspect you already knew that."

With his hands on his knees, he took a few
deep breaths, trying to stabilize his surroundings.

The transition had been jarring. He focused on the streetlight at the end of the alley, imprinting its shape and its white glare in his mind.

"Are you sure you're going to be OK?" Hanh said.

"I just need to walk around a little." He straightened up.

"Come inside."

She led him through the heavy back door of her salon, into the storeroom, then slammed it behind them.

"Do you want a coffee or something?"

"I think I'm all right. I'm just a little disoriented."

"Hang on to the here-now," she said. "Focus on it. Don't think about where you've been for a while."

"That's good advice," he said, and forced a smile.

"Things are a little different now," she said. "I hope it was worth it. I hope the changes aren't too much for you."

"What's changed?"

"Not a lot, but some things."

"Is it like little things all over the place," Mason said, "or specific things in one place?"

Hanh raised her eyebrows. "You'll find out. You're the only person in this world who's seen it both ways."

"Besides you."

"Of course," she said, and waved a hand. "Besides me."

She likely hadn't included herself, Mason thought, because she didn't really qualify as in this world. Hanh was outside it, or straddling this one and others. But that didn't matter right now. He needed to focus on being here, making himself real here.

"You'll be fine," she said, as if reading his thoughts.

She walked out into the dim salon, toward the front door. Mason followed, and as she unlocked it to let him out, he mumbled, "Good night."

Walking across the empty parking lot, toward the sidewalk on Sunset, he realized he had no way to get home, and no phone to call a ride. Digging in his pocket, he had less than a dollar in old coins—nowhere near enough for bus fare. Walking wouldn't be so bad, he decided, even though he was tired, and wearing a suit. The rhythm of pounding the pavement would help him get stabilized.

Close to an hour later, walking up the hill, his head had started to throb. It might be from the lack of caffeine and the time shift, but more likely it was a side effect of being yanked back here. Peggy's familiar car was parked on the street. That was a good sign—it hadn't changed.

The spare key was under the rock near the front door, right where they kept it. That was comfortingly familiar as well.

The living room was dark when he stepped in, although someone had left on the night light over the stove for him. Peggy's door was closed, and the gap under it was dark. His own bedroom door was ajar, and in the ambient light from the windows, Ned's sleeping form was visible under the covers. He paused to take a breath. Ned was here. Mason quietly ditched his suit in the bottom of the closet, then went to shower, and popped some ibuprofen.

When he climbed into bed, Ned rolled toward him and draped an arm across his belly.

"You were out late," he murmured.

"Psychic connections are strongest at night."

Ned scoffed, and Mason soon drifted toward sleep. Things here hadn't changed. What a relief.

IN RECOVERY MODE, MASON slept late, and it was almost eleven when he finally woke. The house was quiet, with Ned and Peggy gone, and as he wandered around, nothing looked different. In the fridge he even recognized the leftover rotini from the other night.

Once he'd made a pot of espresso, he sat at the counter and looked through his phone. Ned and Peggy were still there, and his other contacts seemed intact.

Hanh had implied that there was no way to determine what had changed outside his own memory. He widened his search, reading the news, but it was all familiar, all contiguous with what he remembered. Whatever changes Geraldine's survival had wrought, they didn't seem to be personal to Mason, or about geopolitics, or music, or cinema.

He ate a bowl of muesli, and browsed some more online, and made another pot of coffee. Behind him he heard the front door open, and Ned's familiar voice called out a greeting. Mason slid off his stool and went to embrace him.

"Such a passionate welcome," Ned said.

"It feels like I haven't seen you for a while. You had meetings today?"

"Nope—I had to go to Long Beach to buy floor wax for my linoleum polishing business."

Mason ran a hand through his own hair and took a breath. "Linoleum polishing?"

Ned's eyes narrowed. "Of course I had meetings today. What else would I be doing on Monday morning? I'm sure I told you that."

"I guess you must have. So you're not polishing floors?"

"You thought I started a side business and forgot to mention it until right now?"

"You're the one who said it." Mason gestured helplessly. "Things like that happen all the time in my world."

Ned stifled a sigh. "I was just messing with you. I guess that can be a little fraught. How about pesto and gnocchi for dinner later?"

Once Ned went to his office, and Mason had made a third pot of espresso, he took his mug and his phone out onto the balcony, and spent the afternoon lounging and reading, letting this place sink in. The sun was well into the west when Peggy stepped outside. She was wearing jeans and a T-shirt.

"You're not dressed for school," he said.

"This week is spring break." Dropping into one of the other chairs, she leaned toward him, and spoke in a low voice. "So how did last night go?"

"You remember what I was doing?"

"Of course I remember. One of your bleed-throughs to the 1950s."

"I managed to get Geraldine to the saucer meet-up. She didn't get stuck in the desert that day."

Her brow furrowed. "Now you're confusing me."

"That's why I went back. To help Geraldine."

"Who's Geraldine?"

"I guess it makes sense that you don't know

about her. I told you about Geraldine when we went to Landers last weekend—I stopped her from making a mistake. I gave her a little nudge, and now I'm the only person who remembers how it was before."

"Where's Landers?" Peggy demanded. "I was here all weekend, and so were you. Until last night."

Mason took a breath. "This is getting confusing."

"Of course it is. You're messing with history. What did you expect?"

He gestured helplessly. "Until right now I hadn't come across anything that's different."

"So what became of this woman back then, after you met her?"

"I'm not sure."

"Do you know her surname? Didn't you look for her online?"

Mason stared at her for a moment. "Why didn't I think of checking on that?"

"I can't believe you didn't." She stood up. "Drink some more of that coffee. I'm going to sous-chef for Ned."

Maybe he was still a little dazed—it was the first thing he should have looked for. Thumb-typing Geraldine's name into his phone, he found there were a lot of people with that name, but one of the first on the list made his pulse quicken:

Geraldine Reed, cofounder of the Saucer Institute. Clicking through to the organization's website, he found a photo of her—a portrait, posed and looking into the camera, with a smile on her face. She was much older, and her hair had gone gray, but the eyes were the same.

Mason stared at the screen. He'd done it— Geraldine had survived that long-ago trip, and she'd lived into old age. He read her bio:

> Reed started visiting the high desert in the 1950s, attending some of the early contactee events at Giant Rock and reporting on the movement for newspapers in Los Angeles and later nationwide. Although she never had her own encounters with the visitors from space, in 1960 she and two contactees founded the Saucer Institute, operating near Giant Rock at a ranch that grew into today's campus. Officially retired from her role at the institute, Reed remains active in the organization as leader emerita.

If this was up-to-date, Geraldine was still alive today. She'd lived, and she'd built something, and she hadn't managed to create a black hole to crush the planet, like Peggy had suggested might happen.

Ned opened the door and poked his head out. "Dinner's ready."

Inside he found Matt sitting at the kitchen counter, and greeted him as Ned and Peggy set out plates on the dining table. The pesto was sublime, as always, and they all complimented Ned on it.

"So my colleague Valentina has a house in the Mojave," Matt said. "I thought we could all go out there for a night or two."

"Didn't we already do that?" Mason said.

"Not with me." Matt gestured with his fork. "Wouldn't it be great to get a break from this crazy fucking city?"

"Where in the Mojave?" Ned said.

"It's in Landers. Near the saucer campus. Lots of desert wildland all around. Valentina says it's just over two hours' drive from town."

"Landers," Peggy said flatly, and eyed Mason, her brow furrowing. "Where have I heard that before?"

Mason shrugged and looked away. It was too complicated to explain to her now, especially with Ned sitting there.

Ned waved a hand. "What's the saucer campus?"

"It's a UFO research center, or a retreat center, or both," Matt said. "Run by the Saucer Society or the Saucer League. Something like that."

"It's the Saucer Institute," Mason said.

"Maybe we can leave the paranormal stuff out of it," Ned said, eyeing him. "I get enough exposure to that in everyday life."

Peggy waved dismissively. "Forget all that. I

say we do it. I'm off this week, and so is Matt."

Mason looked from her to Matt, then Ned. The conversation was an eerie echo of the first time they'd gone, just a few weeks ago for him. He could almost feel reality rearranging itself around him to fit the changes he'd made.

"We could go tomorrow," Ned said. "Less traffic than on the weekend."

"Does the psychic world need Mason to be in town this week?" Matt said, raising his eyebrows.

"Things have been slow," Mason said absently. It felt like he was reciting a script, repeating someone else's words. "I can go tomorrow."

After they'd eaten, he volunteered to clean up. Ned went down to his office, and Peggy and Matt disappeared into her room. Working in the kitchen, he thought about how things were different, how they were the same. He remembered Valentina's cabin in the desert, but focusing on it now, it felt like it was starting to fade, like a dream. Standing at the sink with a saucepan in hand, he paused and closed his eyes for a moment, and took a slow breath, willing himself to retain it, to keep those memories clear and intact and real.

"Are you OK?" It was Ned, standing behind him, in the kitchen doorway, come to refill his water glass.

"Just tired," he said, and went back to cleaning the pan.

Later, when he climbed into bed with Ned, before he fell asleep, he cleared his mind and willed psychic insight to suffuse in from the hidden parts of reality. As he sank into the hypnagogic state, the image that came to him was of cloth, loosely woven, like rough burlap, with lumpy threads. The weave was distorted, he saw, thick and rough in places and thinner in others, revealing tiny gaps. But it wasn't broken.

IN THE MORNING MASON found Ned in the kitchen, wearing his stretchy black shirt, doing food prep for their trip. Once he'd eaten breakfast and made a pot of espresso, he took his java and his laptop out onto the balcony. It was still chilly, and he wrapped his hand around the mug for warmth.

He wanted to read more about the Saucer Institute, to make sure it wasn't a nutty religious outfit. Matt had warned him that if Geraldine survived, she might start a cult. Scouring the details online, eventually he was satisfied that it wasn't—the focus of the institute was on academic research and personal development, with the campus operating as a retreat center. Its classes weren't religious and were open to anyone.

Geraldine's personal story blended with those of the other early contactees, but reading more about her, she was always slightly outside it, ostensibly as a journalist, and that gave her the status of an observer rather than a participant. She'd written for newspapers, and later for magazines, and had authored a slew of books with dramatic titles: *Flying Saucers Are Overhead*, and *Big Doings at Giant Rock*, and *What the Space Brothers Really Want*.

A biographer who'd profiled Geraldine in a magazine article a decade ago explained that unlike the other early contactees, she had never spoken about personal encounters with the space brothers. She hadn't set out an agenda for the earthlings, and had never served up political or lifestyle advice, channeled telepathically or otherwise. In the field, that objectivity gave her an elevated position, and she managed to rally financial support for a research project on the UFO phenomena. Over the years that work had morphed into the Saucer Institute.

In the 1970s the Pentagon contracts dried up, the article explained, and the institute had grown more introspective. It held academic retreats and built up its publishing business in addition to supporting pure research. To this day they still did outreach on what the writer called metaphysical thought.

There was another photo of Geraldine in the article, middle-aged and perched in the distinctive rocky landscape around Giant Rock, a sneaker-clad foot propped against a boulder, a confident smile on her face. Just seeing her older than when they'd met made him smile too.

Mason folded his computer closed and went inside. Ned was working on filling the cooler—it was almost time to leave. In the bedroom he pulled on his jeans and a plaid shirt, and threw some clothes into a bag, and remembered to grab his own straw hat, so he wouldn't have to borrow Valentina's.

He carried his bag out to the living room and set it by the door. When Matt arrived, he helped Ned take the cooler out to the car, and Mason went to the kitchen counter, where Peggy was loading the food box.

"You should probably leave the half bottle of prosecco," he said.

She frowned. "Why?"

"It might leak in the trunk."

"I guess that's possible. I'd hate to be held responsible for sullying the Crown Vic." She took the bottle to the fridge. "I'll swap it for an unopened one."

When they finally piled into the Crown Vic, in the same positions as last time, Mason's feeling of déjà vu only increased. Ned's calm driving and even some of the topics of conversation were identical. It was relentless, and uncomfortable, and he knew he could will himself to forget the other version, to immerse himself fully in this moment. But he didn't want that—he wanted to hang on to the memories, to be able to assess what had shifted.

The road up to Valentina's house had the same sandy patch, and Ned powered through it in the same way. The house looked exactly the way he remembered it too. When they carried their bags and the food inside, Peggy went into the hallway to check out the bedrooms.

"Dibs on the one with the Joshua tree out the window," she called. When she came out to the main room, she eyed Mason. "You already put your stuff in the other bedroom."

"I knew which one you'd pick," Mason said.

"Either I'm incredibly predictable, or your psychic power is cranked up to eleven." She frowned. "Wait—have you been here before?"

Mason gestured helplessly.

"You are such a weirdo," she hissed.

Mason laughed. "I definitely have some weird experiences."

After dinner, again with the intense echo of last week, they sat outside to gaze at the stars. Peggy pointed out a satellite, and a few minutes later, another.

"There's so many of them," Ned said.

"It's those internet connectivity ones," she

said. "They keep launching them in fleets."

They chatted about the satellites, and how they reflected the sunlight, and eventually Peggy and Ned went inside. Mason stayed out with Matt, content to be under the sea of stars.

"There's another one," Matt said, waving vaguely at the air. "Wait—there's two of them. They're in formation."

"They seem to travel in swarms," Mason said, watching the bright points drift across the sky.

Then one of the points stopped moving.

"What the fuck?" Matt demanded.

"Weird, right?"

"It can't be a satellite. Or maybe it's an optical illusion—a satellite that flew out of the sunlight, like Peggy said, and what we're staring at is just a star that happened to be in the same place."

"Maybe."

"Or it's because we're right up the road from the Saucer Institute. It attracts the UFO action."

"Hanh says it's stress on the fabric of reality," Mason said. "Like the weave being stretched and pulled apart. Weird things leak through."

"She ought to know."

From the corner of his eye Mason saw movement down the road. It was a pair of pale-blue orbs in the distance, floating over the landscape.

"Take a look," he said, and gestured to the road.

"What the actual fuck?" Matt said, twisting around in his chair.

"It's not flashlights or drones or swamp gas, so don't even go there. Those are totally paranormal."

"Should we go check it out?"

"Of course we should."

Mason got up and led the way around the house. They walked up the road, watching the lights drift slowly across the landscape.

"You seem awfully calm," Matt said, his tone hushed.

"This kind of thing isn't totally unexpected out here. The saucer-heads said Landers is an earth energy vortex."

"I guess that's why they built their institute here."

Farther up the road, they stopped walking, and stood in silence to watch the orbs. Their color shifted from blue to pale orange, and then a pair of round yellow lights appeared, rising above the road in the distance.

"Who the fuck would be driving up here at this hour?" Matt said. "The only house on this road is Valentina's. Do you think it's the military stalking those orbs?"

"That's not a car."

"How do you know that?"

"The lights are too dim, and too flat. No way are those headlights."

The lights rose slightly, and drifted sideways, over the landscape, toward the orbs. It was an eerie repeat of what he'd seen before with Ned.

"Fucking royal fuck," Matt muttered. "You're right."

Eventually all the lights winked out.

"That might be the end of it," Mason said.

He wondered if the spotlight would appear above them, as it had last time, and he stood there, looking up at the sky. But it didn't happen. There were only the stars above. Maybe that brilliant blinding light had been specifically connected to Ned, a response to his skeptical energy. Maybe it was a directed message that he should wake up and accept this stuff as valid. Unfortunately it wasn't going to open Ned's mind—in this world, that incident had never happened.

"I think you're right," Matt said. "It's over."

As they started walking back toward the house, Mason's heart was still pounding.

Sixteen

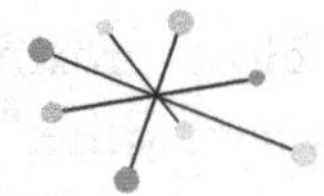

THE NEXT MORNING, WHEN he woke, Mason remembered that aroma.

"Scrambled tofu," he said, walking into the main room.

Peggy looked up from the stove. "How did you know?"

"I can smell it. It's totally tantalizing."

Ned stood at the counter, slicing a red bell pepper. "You're smelling the black salt and the shallots," he said.

Mason poured himself a coffee and joined Matt at the dining table. He was absorbed in his phone, but looked up when Mason sat across from him.

"I was reading about the Saucer Institute and paranormal activity," Matt said. "Technically they don't take credit for UFO sightings and orbs."

"That seems restrained of them. It would be easy to claim it."

"They're actually having an open house today. Any interest?"

"Definitely," Mason said. "Let's go."

"I live in such close proximity to the metaphysical realm in everyday life," Ned said. "I wake up next to it every morning. I'm on vacation here. I want to go hiking and look at the Joshua trees."

"I might stick with that too," Peggy said. "Flying saucers sound like something for the paranormal boys."

"You people have no freaking imagination," Matt said.

Peggy and Ned came over with plates of food and sat with them.

"So the psychics will go expand their minds," Mason said, "while the psychos go stumble around in the desert."

"I just made you breakfast," Peggy said, and shot him a look.

"You really shouldn't trash-talk the guy who has the car keys either," Ned said, "unless you were planning on walking to the institute."

Mason smiled sweetly. "Beloved, may I borrow your car?"

"Of course, *mi vida*." Ned dug in his pocket and handed him the keys. "Don't slow down when you hit that sandy stretch on the road, or you'll get stuck."

After they'd eaten, Matt and Mason headed out in the Crown Vic. Mason drove, and dutifully hit the sandy patch at a decent speed, and managed to plow through it.

The Saucer Institute was on a paved road, just a few miles from Valentina's place, and not really near Giant Rock. The campus was an array of low buildings, interspersed with cacti and majestic Joshua trees. Everything was painted pinky-tan and brown to blend in with the sandy landscape.

A dozen cars were in the dirt parking lot, and the doors of the nearest building were propped open. When they stepped inside, they found a rustic foyer with a reception desk and several small groups of people hanging around.

A woman approached them and recited a perfunctory welcome, then added, "Geraldine Reed is about to speak in the lecture hall. You're also welcome to wander the grounds. We have exhibits set up in some of the other buildings."

"I'd like to hear her speak," Mason said.

The woman pointed out a set of doors, and he and Matt followed several other people inside. It was a small theater, clad in lots of warm pinewood that gave it a rustic vibe. It felt like a high school auditorium that hadn't been renovated since the 1960s. About a third of the seats were occupied, and Mason led the way to the front, where they sat a few rows from the stage.

His heart was pounding in anticipation. Would she remember him, or would the few hours they'd spent together be forgotten, rendered insignificant amid her decades of life experiences?

When Geraldine strode onto the stage, he clapped along with everyone. She was dressed simply, in an airy blouse and raw cotton trousers, a loose turquoise necklace on her breast. She beamed and waved in acknowledgment. It was amazing how vital she looked, considering she had to be well into her eighties by now. Age had made her more graceful, Mason decided. Of course she was a different person than the one he'd met so long ago, but he could see the overlap, the root similarities.

Geraldine stood at the lectern and welcomed everyone. Her voice was clear and strong as she explained the goals of the organization, and told some anecdotes about its early days. Filmmakers had worked with the institute to inject realism into their science fiction, she explained, and a visit to the campus by the UN Secretary General had lent a lot of legitimacy. The institute had kept his secret, that he was a contactee, until a biographer revealed that fact later, well after his death.

Watching her speak, Mason could see the lifetime of wisdom that she'd accrued. Changing her trajectory that day had been worth the risk—he knew that now. Hanh must have known this would be the outcome. It wasn't about schooling him or highlighting his hubris. She'd helped him because she tacitly approved of the revisions.

Maybe Hanh was just letting him experiment. If Matt's idea was accurate, that there were other threads, multiple iterations of reality, maybe all he'd done was to reconnect a single strand where Geraldine existed to his own reality. Somewhere else things were the same as they had been before, and this was just one potential version of many.

Whatever the reason, it made him happy to be here listening to her. A practiced speaker, Geraldine looked at everyone in the room, meeting their gaze. When she spotted Mason, she held his eye a little longer than the others. Was that a spark of recognition?

Before long, she wound up her talk. "So buy a membership, and come to one of our retreats," she said. "There's a lot more happening here than flying saucers."

The crowd gave her a hearty round of applause, and Geraldine descended from the stage to glad-hand her guests. People were on their feet now, and some wandered out to the foyer, while others crowded around the leader emerita.

"Should we go walk around?" Matt said.

"I kind of want to talk to her. I'll catch up."

Mason hung back, in the aisle, and saw that even as she connected with people, Geraldine was scanning the other faces. When she spotted him, there was definitely recognition in her eyes.

Mason shoved his hands into the pockets of his jeans and waited. As the crowd thinned out, Geraldine made her way over to talk to him.

"I think I may have known your grandfather," she said.

"I doubt that, Geraldine."

She frowned. "Have we met?"

"Indeed we have." He pressed his palm to his chest. "It's Mason. I caught a ride with you once."

"You look so very familiar."

"I know you're metaphysically minded," he said, "so I'll be honest with you, because I know you can handle it. I came with you on one of those early trips you made out here from the city. The summer of 1953. You were driving a dark-red Packard."

"That was a lifetime ago. I remember your face, and your voice, but given your age, I know you weren't even born yet." Her brow furrowed. "So you can understand why I'm confused."

"I would be too." Mason waved his arm. "Do

you remember when the radiator overheated near Morrow Field? I walked over to the hangar to get antifreeze."

"You could have read that story in my memoir."

"I guess that's possible. I haven't read your memoir. Did it say how you flirted with me, and that I told you that your roommate, Julia, was into you?"

Her eyebrows shot up. "You knew I was involved with her. I remember that. I couldn't figure out how you knew. I thought maybe you were an FBI plant."

Mason laughed. "I'm not a G-man, then or now."

"How is it that you haven't aged a day?"

"I was just visiting you there. I'm from here."

Standing a few feet away, a woman cleared her throat, and when Geraldine looked toward her, the woman shot her a pointed look.

"I have guests to attend to," Geraldine said, "but I'd like to talk more with you. Can you join me here after dinner?"

"I'll do that," Mason said, and smiled, then walked toward the foyer to look for Matt.

"Somebody made an impression," Matt said. He was standing near the doors of the auditorium. "She's too damn old for you."

Mason waved him outside. "There's more to

it. I met her before."

"Your bleed-through."

"I told you about that, huh."

"Of course you did," he said, squinting as they stepped out into the bright daylight. "You thought I might have to help out. Don't you remember?"

"Things have changed." Mason waved to the other buildings on the campus. "Do you want to walk around?"

"We can just go," he said, and they headed back to the car. "So what's changed?"

"Well, the Saucer Institute wasn't here before."

"Oh, man—what the fuck did you do? The guy I talked to outside said it's been here since the 1960s."

"It feels like it has, but this is all new to me." Mason climbed in behind the wheel of the Crown Vic. "Only to me, though. Everyone else remembers it."

"What else has changed?"

"Nothing that I've noticed. Although the history of the early contactees and the space brothers seems a little different." As he nosed the car out of the parking lot and turned onto the road, he explained Geraldine's original story.

"I can't believe you were able to change that," Matt said finally. "So what was the point of saving her? And why did Hanh go for it?"

"Maybe Geraldine being here is a plus. Maybe

she's enriching the world."

"I think I read one of her books at some point. I'm not sure she qualifies as a great beacon of wisdom."

"What's her writing like?" Mason said.

"As I remember it's about the emotional side of seeing saucers and meeting aliens. How it's an inner experience as well as a mechanical thing."

"Interesting. When I met her, she thought the space brothers were from Venus."

Matt sighed. "I guess if the boss let you do it, there must be a benefit."

When they got back to the house, Ned and Peggy were still off hiking. Mason climbed into the hammock, not really planning to take a nap, but he woke later when Ned came to tell him there were tacos for dinner.

After they'd eaten, Ned said, "Should we sit out under the stars?"

"Someone got invited back to the institute," Matt said, eyeing Mason, "to hang out with the great leader."

Ned frowned. "Who is this guy? Is he trying to get into your pants?"

"It's not a guy," Mason said. "Geraldine Reed is the founder of the institute, and she's in her eighties. She just wants to talk to me."

"Why?" Peggy said.

"Because I'm extremely interesting."

Ned pursed his lips. "I guess you'll find out the real reason when you get there."

Mason scoffed. "I'm going to take your car."

IT WAS DIFFERENT DRIVING in the countryside in the dark. With no streetlights, Mason had to pay close attention to the road. At the institute he parked in the lot and went into the building with the theater, where there was a front desk.

"I have a meeting with Geraldine Reed," he told the clerk.

"You're Mr. Mason?"

"That's right."

She smiled. "Go to building 4. Through these doors and left."

The paths were lit with subtle downlights rather than overhead fixtures, likely to preserve the dark sky and maximize the chance to see flying saucers. Building 4 looked like an oversize cabana, and he stepped up and knocked on the door.

Geraldine opened it for him. She was wearing the same airy cotton as earlier in the day but with a sweater on her shoulders. The interior looked like a hotel suite, with living room furniture, and lots of wood, like Valentina's house. She gestured for him to sit, and he took an easy chair, across the coffee table from where she sat down on the sofa.

"My security guy didn't want me to meet with you alone," she said.

"I guess I should feel honored."

"I told him we were old friends."

Mason smiled. "I feel that way too."

"I'd like you to explain what's going on," she said, and held his gaze. "You kind of rattled me today."

"I didn't intend to do that. I saw that you recognized me."

"How is it that you look the same as you did that day?"

"I have the ability to bleed through to the past," Mason said. "I use it in my research sometimes."

"What kind of research do you do?"

"I'm a psychic investigator."

She waved a hand. "Go on."

"I can project to the recent past just using my mind. To go farther, though, and to take my body with me, I need help from other psychics. It takes a gestalt of psychic energy."

"I've never heard of that before. How did you develop this ability?"

"The first time it happened," Mason said, "I had a run-in with an extraterrestrial artifact. That happened near here, actually—closer to Victorville. It knocked me flat and sent me forty years into the past."

She sat forward. "What kind of artifact?"

"It was a little piece of metal. I knew it was something different by the way it felt. Like a piece of waxy foil."

"Do you still have it?"

"When I got back, it was gone."

"Over the years I've seen plenty of evidence of crashed saucers. One of the perks of being prominent in the field is that people trust me with things. But I've never seen anything with that kind of power." Her eyes narrowed. "As strange as it is, however, I can't deny the evidence right in front of me."

Mason nodded. "Then we're on the same page."

"If you're from here, why did you come to see me that day?"

"I read an article about the early meet-ups at Giant Rock," he said, and explained how she'd become lost in the desert.

Geraldine sat back and shook her head. "It's just so hard to believe."

"Maybe that's OK," he said, and watched her for a moment. "I know it's a lot. You don't have to buy into it. It doesn't change anything."

"Still—I want to understand."

"Do you remember me convincing you where to turn off the main road to get to Landers? You wanted to go farther east."

"I don't remember that."

"But you remember me. When I approached you the day before, I told you that the super at your apartment, a guy named Parker, had told me about your trip. In reality I already knew about it from the old newspaper stories."

"You're saying that you saved my life."

"I don't think that's what happened," Mason said. "I think you decided to save your own life. More accurately, you decided to pick another path through reality. The one you're on now. I just gave you a nudge that day. I pointed out the options. Maybe I convinced you to take the correct turn, but you're the one who made the turn."

"I suspect it was more than a single turn, or a single nudge."

"Maybe," Mason said. "Maybe we can call it a psychic nudge."

Also from Dagmar Miura

The Mason Braithwaite Paranormal Mystery Series

No one is ever quite sure whether psychic investigator Mason gets results with actual psychic power or his more mundane flatfooting, but the disheveled redhead manages to resolve some intractable mysteries.

mason.dagmarmiura.com

Penstock Canyon

While helping out a friend suffering from late-night visitations, psychic investigator Mason is confronted with aliens on the roof and other liminal beings that have him questioning the very nature of reality.

mason.dagmarmiura.com

The Slater Ibáñez Books

Don't mess with the hothead, or he might just mess with you. The first book in the series sees the insurance investigator running surveillance on an injured tech worker and tangling with blackmailers, party girls, late-night hookups with a gamut of guys, and a lot of bourbon.

slater.dagmarmiura.com

Brawl in Bardo

Slater spends the night in a dusty Mojave Desert town and finds that things look different in the space between LA and Vegas, like the bardo between lives. Soon he's stalking a sleazy dermatologist who's in a custody battle with another croaker for a seemingly worthless statue.

slater.dagmarmiura.com

Truman and Celeste

Sometimes all a woman needs is a decent man—even if she's not sleeping with him. Join Truman and Celeste as they troll the gritty underbelly of Los Angeles, never hesitating to slam that cocktail, hit on guys, or ask the next relevant question.

truman.dagmarmiura.com

The Cape Cod Blue

The glittering, exalted world of art auctioning hides love, hate, and parricidal murder in a wealthy and socially prominent family when forgery of an anonymous Cape Cod painting is used to steal a world-famous portrait that's worth a fortune.

capecod.dagmarmiura.com

The Bone Bridge

Yarrott Benz, the 2016 Ippy Award winner for memoir, is forced to deal with extraordinary self-sacrifice in this harrowing account of teenage brothers, as different as night and day, trapped together in a dramatic medical dilemma.

bonebridge.dagmarmiura.com

The Psychic Vegan Cookbook

It has never been easier to cook vegan, and you don't even need to be psychic to do it. Whether your motivation is eating healthier or the welfare of other sentient creatures, Henrietta Flores guides you through plant-based versions of familiar dishes.

cookbook.dagmarmiura.com

9 781951 130473